There was something too realistic in the way the actress's body melted into the actor's, and in the way her arms clung around his neck as if she lacked the strength to support herself.

They moved apart to stand staring at each other, breathing heavily. "What was that all about?" Persey finally managed to ask, using all her professional technique in an attempt to sound affronted.

"I felt I had to make it convincing."

"I see." Her voice was icy.

"I'll not deny that I enjoyed every second of it. And unless I mistake the matter, so did you. . . ."

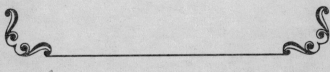

By Marian Devon
Published by Fawcett Books:

LORD HARLEQUIN

Marian Devon

FAWCETT CREST • NEW YORK

A Fawcett Crest Book
Published by Ballantine Books
Copyright © 1994 by Marian Pope Rettke

Library of Congress Catalog Card Number: 94-94399

ISBN 0-449-22279-9

Manufactured in the United States of America

First Edition: December 1994

10 9 8 7 6 5 4 3 2 1

Chapter One

"PICCOLO! PICCOLO! PICCOLO!"

The chant was accompanied by a thunder of stamping feet. Then, in response, a clown somersaulted downstage to land with straddled legs and arms akimbo.

"Are we here again?"

His mouth split into a rapturous grin, wide enough for the red lips to join the red triangles painted upon his whitened cheeks. A red cockade gyrated upon his bald-pate wig. He surveyed the crowd with rolling eyes. His toes turned in. He quivered with excitement. The frills and flounces and patches of his multicolored costume were set in frenzied motion.

"How are you tomorrow?" he asked the audience. And they clapped their hands in rhythm with their shouted comeback:

"Piccolo! Piccolo! Piccolo!"

Sadler's Wells Theatre was sold out. Just as it had been every night in that summer season. For London was deserting the legitimate stage in droves to make the journey to Islington and be entertained by ballets and burlesques, by juggling and tumbling, by tightrope walkers and singers and dancers and animal acts. But the real draw was the Pantomime. And England's greatest clown.

All eyes (with the exception of one bright blue pair) were now glued upon Piccolo. They applauded as he launched into one of his famous "turns," singing lustily

> My first wife's dead
> There let her lie.
> She's at rest
> And so am I. . . .

The audience clutched their aching sides as the clown's funereal expression alternated with delight. The finer nature of the conscience-stricken widower fought hard. But no sooner would he achieve a suitably tragic expression than glee would get the upper hand, to the delight of a roaring audience.

Behind him on the stage, Harlequin, that stock figure of the Pantomime, watched intently, his expression matching the clown's rapidly changing moods. But the attention of the third member of the trio, pretty Columbine, had wandered. It was fastened upon one particular stage box that had drawn it like a magnet for the past two nights.

One member of its party—the host, she judged—was all too familiar. Colonel Hartland, a once-handsome man now running to paunch and thinning hair, had been casting lures her way for several weeks. He was, so he avowed, a great devotee of the Pantomime. Most who knew him, though, would have said that his real devotion was to the attractive young women who performed in that entertainment. This season he had singled out Columbine for his special attention, a state of affairs that she could have done without.

But her eyes swept past the colonel's leer. Nor did they pause to study the rather personable young man on his left or the dazzling beauty on his other side. They quickly found their intended target. And her shapely, darkened brows knitted into a frown.

Just why this particular gentleman had this particular magnetic effect was past Columbine's understanding. True, he was striking looking, with hair almost as fair as his white cambric shirt and with eyes and eyebrows dark as coal in contrast. High cheekbones and a cleft in his well-molded chin gave his face distinction. But it was not his good looks that had obsessed the actress. The world of the theater was, after all, awash with handsome men (though hardly wellborn ones like this obvious nob). No, it was his rapt attention that intrigued her. And the fact that not a bit of it was directed toward her.

Columbine (though she knew her place as supporting character to the Wells's true star) was accustomed to receiving more attention than she really cared for from young and not-so-young gentlemen. They might come to the theater to see the celebrated Piccolo, but it was her dressing room that was crowded afterward.

But this member of the ton seemed impervious to her charms (directed, of course, at Harlequin but carefully angled to give that particular stage box full benefit). She had batted the long, thick lashes that gave her blue eyes added luster. She had pouted her pretty rouged mouth. Then with a sudden shift of mood she had displayed the dimples in her heart-shaped face. She had tossed her head coquettishly, shaking the ringlets of her raven hair. She had shrugged her bare white shoulders to the peril of her décolletage. Nothing. Oh, other males in the audience went wild, of course, whistling and sighing and hooting and acting like perfect jinglebrains. But there was no reaction whatsoever from the annoying gentleman with the flaxen hair. He spent every minute of the Pantomime leaning perilously over the stage box rail, his eyes intent upon Piccolo.

He seemed mesmerized by the clown's performance. Even when the attention should have been upon the lesser characters, his eyes never left the star as he studied Piccolo's reaction to the interplay of Columbine and Harlequin.

Well, she had heard of such men, of course. Those who showed little or no interest in the opposite sex. And come to think on it, the beauty beside him had made no headway either in claiming his attention. But just then the young lady leaned over to whisper something in his ear and the gentleman turned toward her and smiled. The actress felt an irrational stab of jealousy.

"Columbine!"

The hiss came from the star of Sadler's Wells. Piccolo's back was to the audience and there was fury in his eyes. For the first time in her professional life, Columbine had missed a cue. She brought her hands up to her rouged cheeks in exaggerated coyness, dipped a pert curtsy to the clown, then ran shrieking in circles around the stage while he pursued her with mock lasciviousness.

The crowd crowed its delight as Piccolo halted in mid-chase to walk downstage and pantomime, with a wicked grin, what he meant to do, when—and if—he succeeded in catching the agile beauty.

Possibly the only member of the theater audience who realized that Columbine had missed her cue was an occupant of the stage box directly opposite the one that had caused all the problems. Lady Lavinia Pickering was playing hostess to her cousin, Adelaide Oliver, and to their longtime bosom bow, Jane Abingdon.

The Pantomime would not have been Lady Lavinia's choice of entertainment. She would have much preferred attending the legitimate offerings of those licensed theaters, Covent Garden and Drury Lane. But it was Addie's birthday (her fiftieth, a milestone her friends had reached a few months earlier) and, therefore, Addie's choice. And she had preferred a visit to the Pantomime "above all things."

But in actuality, Lady Lavinia, who had come expecting to be bored, had found the evening surprisingly diverting. First of all, she had developed a genuine, if grudging, respect for Piccolo. After all, an artist was an artist, whether declaiming the Bard's immortal lines or keeping numerous colored balls successfully in the air while prancing dizzily upon a tightrope.

But it wasn't the performance that most interested her ladyship. For the founder of the Pickering Club, formed to expand its female members' horizons, was a dedicated student of human nature. And she had not missed Columbine's fascination with the theater party across the pit from them.

Indeed, when the three ladies had first arrived,

that particular box had also captured their attention. "Oh, look." Addie had nudged her cousin as the threesome scanned the theater with their opera glasses. "There. Directly across. It's Colonel Hartland's party. And you said just the hoi-polloi would be here."

"I said nothing of the kind."

"Well, then you thought it."

Lady Lavinia had not bothered to deny this accusation. She had merely studied the colonel's party thoughtfully, joined in the pursuit by her closest friends.

Their friendship dated all the way back to childhood, when the threesome had met at a fashionable boarding school. It had continued unabated through the marriages and widowhood of Adelaide and Jane and the determined spinsterhood of her ladyship. Then and now, Lady Lavinia had been the bear-leader of the triumvirate.

Nature had fitted her for the role. She was tall, with a narrow face and an aristocratic nose. She had jet black eyes with hair that matched them, despite the advancing years. (Her friend Jane declared that Lavinia kept the gray away by an act of iron will, whereas other lesser mortals were doomed to dye.)

Few would have ever guessed that Adelaide Oliver was Lady Lavinia's cousin. Nature seemed bent upon illustrating heredity's variety. Addie was small and thin (skinny, the uncharitable might say), with light brown graying hair, ingenuous blue eyes, and a rabbity temperament.

Their friend Jane Abingdon, known by their intimates, to her dismay, as "the sensible one," was plump and pretty, with fine gray eyes and waving hair that matched them most becomingly.

The three friends' perusal of the audience had ended with Piccolo's dramatic entrance. But the subject was still on Addie's mind at the intermission.

"She is every bit as lovely as they say," she sighed as the curtain closed.

"Well, it goes with the role, does it not?" Jane answered practically. "There would be no point in casting an antidote as Columbine. They would never make an audience believe she could create all that havoc. Of course," she mused, "I have seen actresses quite long in the tooth who managed to—"

"No, no. Not her," Adelaide interrupted quite impatiently. "I am speaking of Colonel Hartland's daughter, Pamela." She gestured with her fan across the pit. "They say she was the sensation of this past Season, with gentlemen simply swarming after her. And it is easy to see why."

Three pairs of glasses studied Miss Hartland thoughtfully.

"Hmmm. Looks a bit vapid to me" was Lady Lavinia's pronouncement. "But then, I collect that gentlemen rarely look for character in a female."

"Not when confronted with golden ringlets, limpid eyes, and flawless skin and features," Jane chuckled. "That would be asking a bit much of your average gentleman."

"Oh, Miss Hartland did not need to settle for an *average* gentleman," literal-minded Adelaide chimed in. "They say she had her pick of the most eligible men about town. Even the Earl of Atwater, who has resisted all the lures cast at him for donkey's years, made a complete cake of himself. But she had eyes only for Lord Worth."

The opera glasses shifted. "Well *he* seems to have eyes for other things," Lavinia observed dryly as

7

they studied the fair-haired young man. "I have never seen anyone so intent upon a performance. Tell me, who is the other young man in their party? I would have wagered that he was the one smitten by Miss Hartland."

"Oh, he undoubtedly is. Is that not what I was just saying?"

"I collect that must be one of the Warrens," Jane decided. "You remember Caroline Findlater from school, do you not? She married Sir Malcomb Warren and produced numerous offspring. I have met this young man, but for the life of me cannot recall his name. The heir is called Adolphus, God help him. But I do not—"

This exercise in genealogy was cut short by Piccolo's arrival back upon the stage in a whirl of handsprings. As always, his entrance was accompanied by a deafening roar.

"Piccolo! Piccolo! Piccolo!"

Adelaide and Jane were immediately swept up into the action. Their friend, however, was not so easily seduced. True to the spirit of the Pickering Club, she continued to study the strange interplay between the occupants of the opposite box and the onstage characters. She was, therefore, privy to the fact that once again Columbine had become distracted by the Hartland party and had missed another cue.

Lavinia was not, of course, privy to the onstage scene that took place immediately after the curtain fell, when Piccolo turned the full force of his pent-up wrath upon the female lead. "Miss McCall," he barked, "I will see you immediately in my dressing room!"

"Yes, sir," Columbine replied contritely.

But the interchange would have come as no surprise to her ladyship.

Chapter Two

THE GAMESTERS IN WHITE'S CLUB FOR GENTLEMEN were oblivious to time. Therefore, when Lord Worth and his cousin, Mr. Warren, ambled into the card room after driving all the way from Islington, they had no difficulty in finding a game.

They were soon forced to question their luck, however. For it quickly became apparent that the two gentlemen who had relinquished their seats were motivated not so much from a professed desire to try their fortune at faro as from the fact that one of the whist players, Sir Dibdin Kirby, was well on his way to becoming thoroughly disguised.

Sir Dibdin, while amiable enough when sober, was notorious for his change of disposition when in his cups. Once he had passed his limit, he quickly moved from surly to irascible, then on to belligerent. The newcomers learned to their sorrow that he had crossed that Rubicon some time before.

Lord Worth, an accomplished, and sober, whist player, was soon pulling in the lion's share of tricks while Sir Dibdin, who had drawn Clarence Warren for a partner, grew more and more incensed. His glazing eyes could still manage a glare beneath his scowling brow. His pudgy face, cherubic at the best of times, was flushed and angry.

After Lord Worth's partner, Mr. Zachery White, had totaled up the score and money was exchanging hands, Clarence Warren heaved a sigh for his depleted purse. "You do have the devil's own luck, cousin."

"Ha! Luck, you call it," Sir Dibdin growled.

"Luck, certainly." Mr. Warren's eyes had narrowed. The look he gave his partner was not approving. "Would you care to call it anything else?" he challenged.

Smiling amiably, Lord Worth planted a swift kick on his cousin's shin. "Of course he would. He could always mention skill and practice."

"Oh, come now, Worth. No need to act obtuse. Dibdin here was accusing you of cheating."

"Have you lost your mind, Clarence?" Worth hissed out of the corner of his mouth.

"Oh, I am sure he meant no such thing," Mr. White interposed nervously. "Did you Dibdin, old fellow?"

"It just seems deuced odd to me that when the luck has been running my way all evening that Worth sits in and everything turns about. Bound to have been something havey-cavey going on."

Mr. Warren's patience was growing thin. "Could your increased port consumption possibly have had a bearing on the case? It would be a wonder if you could see your cards, let alone play them."

It was the wrong thing entirely to have said. Sir

Dibdin had been lectured upon numerous occasions about his drinking excesses. He had vowed temperance far too often to tally up his failures. The subject was a sore one.

He leaped to his feet. "What I have or have not drunk has nothing to say in the matter!" he shouted as play of all kinds stopped and heads turned their way. "Lord Worth had to have been cheating!"

"And you, sir, are too foxed to know what you are saying," Worth sighed as he pocketed his winnings. "Come on, Clarence."

But as he rose to leave, Sir Dibdin lunged. Mr. Warren quickly stepped between the two.

"Come to your senses, man. Do you want us all barred from here for brawling? If you have a score to settle with my cousin, do it like a gentleman. Pistols at dawn. Zach, you act for him. I'll second Worth."

"I—I don't really think—" Mr. White, by name and nature pale, turned florid. "Not at all the thing. Against the law, actually."

"Good God, Clarence," Worth said, glaring at his cousin, "you must be as foxed as Dibdin."

"Not a bit of it." Warren gave him a speaking look. "It's settled, then. The duel will take place in the park at sunrise. Pistols, of course. A quick word with you, Zach. You, cousin, can wait outside for me."

When Mr. Warren emerged onto St. James's Street a few minutes later, he was confronted by his furious relative. "Of all the chuckle-headed, bird-witted, asinine things to have happened. Have you lost your mind entirely? A duel, for God's sake! Nobody fights duels anymore. And as much as I'd love to draw Dibdin's cork, I've no desire to blow his brains out. Providing he has any, that is."

"Now, now. No need to put yourself into a taking," Mr. Warren said soothingly as they began to stride toward their respective Mayfair residences. "There won't be any duel. You should know that Dibdin won't remember any of this by daylight."

Despite these assurances, it seemed to Worth that he had scarcely crawled into his bed before his cousin was shaking him awake.

"Go away!" Worth sat up in his four-poster and glared.

"Come on, slug-a-bed," Clarence grinned. "We have an appointment to keep, remember?"

"What I remember is that you said Dibdin wouldn't be there."

"What I said was that he most likely wouldn't remember the whole business. But just in case he does show up, you can't have him telling the world that you funked it, now, can you?"

"Why not? I for one don't gave a damn what— My God!" His eyes focused on the black case in his cousin's hands. "You've actually brought pistols."

"That's right. If he is there, it is just as well to put the fear of the Lord into that hothead."

"Get one thing straight, coz. There is no way that I am going to fight a duel."

"We know that, but Dibdin doesn't. If he does show up, first we make him crawl and soothe your injured dignity, then we make him treat us to breakfast at the Unicorn. And if he ain't there, well, you can buy me breakfast for my pains."

"Your pains. It seems to me that if you had not been quite so zealous—well, never mind." Lord Worth heaved himself out of bed. "I'm wide awake now anyway. Are you sure the Unicorn does a decent breakfast? You've never been up before noon in your entire life."

The sun was just peeping above the horizon when they approached the clearing in the wooded, relatively secluded spot selected for the duel. "Well, I can see they came," his lordship sighed as he spied two figures standing knee-deep in the mist rising up from the dew-soaked grass. But as the cousins came closer, they realized that they were much mistaken. The waiting men, dressed in top hats, blue coats, and carrying truncheons, were most assuredly not Sir Dibdin and his second.

"Good God, it's the peelers." Lord Worth was the first to identify the two as members of the newly created London police force.

"I think we'd best be leaving," his cousin whispered. But as they turned to do so, an imperious voice commanded, "Stop in the name of the law!"

The cousins looked at each other, sighed, and capitulated.

"Which of you is Lord Worth?" The taller of the two burly officers barked out the question when they came abreast.

"I am."

"Well then, sir, you are under arrest."

"Now, look here, officer." Worth's voice was placating. "I realize that all this looks rather bad, but I can assure you that we have no real intention of fighting a duel."

"That's true, officer," Warren chimed in, edging the pistol case behind him. As the peeler's eyes followed the movement, he added defiantly, "You can't arrest a cove for what he hasn't done, you know."

"Yes, we do know," the spokesman replied grimly. "Lord Worth"—he turned toward the peer and spoke formally—"I am arresting you, in the king's name, for willfully shooting, with intent to kill—"

"And in the back," his shorter, younger colleague chimed in scornfully.

"One Sir Dibdin Kirby."

"What?" Both young men gaped at the peelers in disbelief.

"But that is impossible." Mr. Warren rallied first. "We just got here."

"So it would appear," the larger officer spoke dryly. "But according to Sir Dibdin's testimony—"

"He's alive, then?" Worth interrupted with relief.

"Yes, Sir Dibdin is in hospital. Alive. At least for now."

"No thanks to some," his colleague muttered darkly.

"Alive and has identified his assailant. It seems that you, Lord Worth, shot from out of that clump of trees." He pointed behind them. "And as he fell he saw you turn and run."

"The devil he did. I haven't been near this place until now."

"That's true, officer. I can vouch for the fact I had to wake him up to come here."

"That is for the courts to decide, sir. My orders are to arrest his lordship here. So come along, sir. I would not like to have to force you."

What happened then was so unexpected that both the peelers—and Lord Worth—were caught completely off their guard. Mr. Clarence Warren wheeled upon the smaller of the two officers. His fist cracked upon the policeman's chin in a leveler that would have done the boxing champion of England credit. "Run, Worth!" he shouted while he executed a flying tackle that brought the larger officer into collision with the turf next to his fallen companion.

Quicker than thought, Lord Worth took to his heels. The larger peeler sprang up and after him, but his cousin had bought him a few seconds' grace, and he was younger and more fit than his pursuer. He raced down Rotten Row and out of the park.

Piccadilly was now teeming with activity. Vendors of shrimps and rosemary, gingerbread and pippins, cherries and sealing wax, impeded his progress. He weaved around an old woman roasting hot codlins upon a fire and almost collided with a little black-faced boy shouting "Chimney sweep! Chimney sweep!" He raced on, while the sound of pursuing boots echoed behind him. Then, when he finally stopped and his gasps of breath subsided to the point where he could hear again, he was no longer being chased.

Worth's first instinct was to turn toward home. But he quickly realized the folly of that course of action. He also rejected the notion of seeking out Sir Dibdin in hospital and asking just what the devil he meant by such a blatantly false charge. He doubted the law would be tolerant enough to allow him to come face-to-face with his accuser.

And he was beginning to regret his flight, realizing that he must now look guilty as sin. He quickly ran through a mental list of his closest friends. No one he could think of, except for Clarence, who now had police problems of his own, would be eager to harbor a fugitive. Well, he could not stand there deliberating all morning. He must choose a course of action.

Lord Worth straightened his cravat and felt a pang of regret for the top hat he had lost in flight that would have largely concealed his distinctive head of hair. He patted his pocket to make sure it still contained his purse, and, after waiting for a mail coach to sweep past, stepped nonchalantly out into the street, where he flagged down a hackney cab.

"Islington," he told the jarvey. "Sadler's Wells Theatre." He started to add that there was a tip in it if he lost no time, but quickly changed his mind. It would not be wise to make the driver think he was in a hurry. He slouched down out of view and tried, unsuccessfully, to make his mind a blank.

When he entered the theater by the stage door, Worth's first impression had been that it was deserted. But then he heard a slight noise and went to peer onstage. A young woman who looked vaguely familiar was touching up the canvas leaves of a faded forest scene. She turned at the sound behind her, gasped out "You!" and dropped the paint pail she was holding.

Mesmerized, the man and woman watched while leaf-green liquid rose in a spectacular arc, then, as gravity had its way, reversed itself to land with an awesome splash and spread in rivulets over the grimy boards.

Chapter Three

WHEN THE MAN WHO OCCUPIED HER THOUGHTS suddenly appeared, Miss McCall's first impression was that she had conjured up a vision.

Those thoughts had admittedly been a muddle. On the one hand, she resented him for being the unwitting cause of her present predicament. On the other hand, she was at a loss to understand her own obsession. That he in his turn had been even more obsessed by Piccolo's performance seemed an inadequate explanation for her state of mind.

"No one is allowed backstage, sir." His class had no monopoly on "haughty."

"I can see why." His eyes followed the traveling paint. "By the bye, do females ordinarily do this type of work?"

"Upon occasion." She was not about to admit that she was being penalized for missing her cue the night before. Piccolo could forgive many things, but

17

not a lapse in professionalism. "Excuse me a moment."

She hurried offstage and returned with a stack of newspapers. As she began mopping up spilled paint, Worth wadded up several sheets of *The Morning Post* and knelt to help her.

"Thank you," she said formally when the job was completed, unaware that a green smudge on the tip of her nose rather undermined the dignity she strove for. "Now then, you really should not be here, you know. The public is not allowed. Didn't Henry tell you so?"

He pulled a snowy white handkerchief from an inside pocket, moistened one corner with his tongue, and applied it to her nose. "Henry?"

"Thank you." She looked at the green mess on the pristine linen and winced. "Henry is the porter. He is supposed to prevent—" She paused and looked disgusted. "But then, I collect he has slipped off to the tavern again."

"Possibly. At least there was no one to challenge me. But I'm not here to make away with any of the stage properties. Actually, I'd like to see Piccolo."

"You don't know much about theater folk, do you?" She stood with her hands on her hips, scornful of such a flat where her profession was concerned.

"Not a lot," he admitted.

"Well, they are not early risers."

"With one exception." He had finally seen beyond the absence of makeup and the fact that she was wearing a protective smock, several sizes too large, over her morning dress. "You are Columbine, are you not?"

She was frankly surprised that he could identify her. And a little bit appeased. "Well, yes. And you

18

might say that, today at least, I am the exception that proves the rule. But as for Piccolo, the best time for you to see him is after the performance tonight."

"My business can't wait that long. Could you tell me where I might find him?"

"I could. But I doubt he would appreciate my doing so. What is your business with him?"

He did not answer "None of yours," but his haughty look implied it. She refused to be overset, however, and waited for an answer.

"I wish to see him about employment," he reluctantly replied.

"About *what*?"

"You heard me, I collect."

"*You* wish employment?" She laughed derisively as she took in his Bond Street attire, the dark blue coat, short-tailed, nipped in at the waist with sleeves that gathered at the shoulders. It was worn with a white waistcoat and gray doeskin trousers. The very latest crack, or she was a Dutchman. "Surely you must be funning."

"I assure you that I am not. Not that I can see why you concern yourself in the matter."

"Oh, but I am concerned. We are one big family here. Just what sort of employment are you seeking?"

"'Well, it is obvious that you are in dire need of a competent person to paint scenery"—he was becoming more than a little nettled by this chit's scorn—"but actually I wish to be a performer."

"A performer!" she choked.

"I say, is there an echo in here somewhere? Now then, Miss Columbine, could you contain your mirth long enough to tell me where I might find Piccolo?"

"Oh, indeed. I'll do better than that, sir. I'll take you to him. I can't wait to hear his reaction, Mr.—?" She looked at him inquiringly.

"Kean. Edmund Kean," he replied icily.

"Very amusing" was her reaction to having the name of London's leading tragedian preempted. "Well, come along now."

Without benefit of any further conversation (the grim set of his mouth did not encourage small talk), she led him outside through the south exit of the building. They crossed the New River over a stone, iron-railed bridge, then walked down a gravel path to a nearby cottage.

Piccolo's house, a square stone edifice with a square-columned portico, boarded several Sadler's Wells performers and was presided over by a notorious busybody who never heard the front door open without checking to see who was going or coming there. Worth's escort gave the middle-aged matron a brief nod, then led him up the staircase that took up most of the entryway's small space. She hurried down the first floor corridor to a doorway at its end and pounded lustily upon the heavy oak.

"Go away!" a muffled voice replied.

She kept up the pounding.

"Who the devil's there?" The angry tone was not encouraging.

The actress gave her companion an impudent grin. "It's me. I've brought Edmund Kean to see you."

There was a pause. Then came the unmistakable sound of bare feet striking floor.

"Oh, thank you for that." Worth glared. "He really will be pleased to see me under these circumstances."

"You mean you aren't actually Edmund Kean?" She threw up her hands in mock surprise as the door was opening.

"What the devil!"

Piccolo, clad in slippers and a bright crimson dressing gown, stood surveying them.

Without his makeup he would have been impossible to recognize as a clown of any sort, let alone England's greatest. In repose, the elastic face was nearly handsome, the features regular with the exception of a too-large mouth. He was of an average height, slightly built, with the acrobat's musculature. His eyes were his outstanding feature, gray and intelligent and penetrating. They now rested upon Lord Worth, sizing him up.

His words, however, were addressed to Worth's companion. "What are you doing here, Persey, at this ungodly hour?"

"Mr. Kean here insisted upon seeing you. Wouldn't take no for an answer. The thing is"— laughter gurgled up—"h-he's looking for employment."

"Is that so?" The eyes now narrowed.

"Yes, sir."

There was a long pause while Piccolo seemed to think the matter over. "In that case," he finally said, "he had best step inside."

Lord Worth took considerable satisfaction from the astonished look on Columbine's face as the clown's bedchamber door closed upon it.

He glanced around him, taking in the canopied bed, the huge mahogany clothes press, the japanned desk, the Adam-style fireplace. It was a typical gentleman's bedchamber except in one respect. The yellow silk wall covering was almost hidden by framed theatrical prints showing Piccolo in the various costumes and antics of his repertoire.

While this quick assessment was going on, the clown's gaze remained fixed upon Worth's face. He did not indicate a chair though two leather upholstered wing-backs were placed near the fireplace. He simply stood waiting for the other man to speak.

Worth found the steady gaze disconcerting. "You couldn't possibly remember me," he began awkwardly, "but we have met before, sir. When I was ten years old. My mother brought me to the Wells as a birthday treat, then took me backstage to meet you."

"As a matter of fact, I do remember. Quite well." The clown spoke dryly; his expression was withdrawn. "And unless I mistake the matter, you have been back once a year ever since. But just this week you have doubled your record and seen the current performance twice."

"You know who I am, then?"

"Who doesn't know the Viscount Worth?" The bow was only slightly mocking but sufficient to arouse an angry flush.

"Don't play games with me, uncle."

The clown shrugged. "Isn't it a bit late to call off the game at this point? After all, it was your family that established the rules. When my sister married a member of the aristocracy, she was forbidden to acknowledge her raffish background. I have played the game successfully for almost thirty years, so why change the rules now?"

"Because I need help and did not know where else to turn for it."

The admission obviously did not come easily. The

clown looked thoughtfully at the desperate face,
then shrugged.

"Well, why not. I am fairly plump in the pocket—
for an actor. Gambling, is it? Don't tell me you've
lost the ancestral pile on the turn of a card. That's
a bit too trite even for the Pantomime." He was
walking toward his desk. "Tell me how much you
need and I'll draw up a voucher for you to sign. You
won't object if I keep this on a businesslike basis?
However, I will not charge you interest, since we
are—er—family." Again, the sarcasm was light.

"Damn your blunt!" Worth spoke angrily. "I'm not
here for a touch. Didn't you listen to—Columbine—
whoever? It's a position that I'm looking for."

The older man turned, his eyebrows raised. "Oh,
I heard all right. But I supposed it was all a hum.
For Miss McCall's benefit. Just what sort of posi-
tion did you have in mind? I don't need a secretary.
I attend to my own affairs."

"I wish to perform."

Worth was growing used to the other's gimlet
gaze, but the bark of laughter that followed his
statement was disconcerting.

"I am glad to furnish so much amusement," he
said stiffly. "The young woman who brought me
here found me equally hilarious."

"The young *lady*," Piccolo emphasized softly.

"I stand corrected."

"The reason for our amusement would not be apparent to a lay person, I collect. But you should
know that although we actors are held in low
esteem—and this is especially true of Pantomime
performers—the fact remains that everything we
do that appears so easy is the result of years and
years of grueling practice. Your grandfather"—he
used the relationship like an insult—"pushed me

23

onstage when I was a toddler, sir, and I have been there ever since."

"And, I, sir, am not the complete imbecile that you appear to take me for. I realize all that. Nor am I ignorant of the family history. I know, for instance, all about the great-grandfather who was famous for his tightrope skills. My mother saw to it that I was well aware that not only the Forsythe blood flowed in my veins. And while no performer can hold a candle to the Great Piccolo"—he copied the other's sneer—"still, one does one's best."

Worth gave a sudden spring, flipped in the air without the aid of hands, and landed with straddled legs and arms akimbo at the clown's feet. "Are we here again?" he parodied.

The clown laughed. Spontaneously. At length. And for the first time in the interview his stage magnetism showed. Worth, who had been seething, could not keep from grinning back.

"Come. Sit down." Piccolo nodded toward the leather chairs. "I'll ring for tea. It always helps my disposition. And, frankly, you look in need of a restorative. Something stronger perhaps?"

"No. Tea will be the very thing."

The housekeeper had anticipated the request, and they were soon settled with a tray containing the tea, Sally Lunn, and a quodeny of plums placed on a card table between them.

"What else can you do?" Piccolo inquired after a few restoring gulps of the steaming beverage.

"Almost everything that you do—badly. I started trying to imitate you after that first birthday performance. It seems I was nine years too late even then," he added wryly. "The results would not have been impressive to your audience, but my schoolmates found them entertaining."

24

"I see." There was a thoughtful pause. "Even so, Lord Worth, I find it difficult to believe that the blood of the performing Piccolos flowing through your veins is forcing you upon the stage. Why this urgent need to perform just now?"

Worth put down his cup to face his uncle squarely. "My urgent need isn't to perform, sir. It is to hide. And a clown's makeup is a marvelous disguise. As you well know. I would never have known you, yet you are one of the most celebrated men of our time. The last place anyone would look for me is on the stage. And while still earning my keep, I would have time enough to do some—necessary investigation."

Piccolo pushed his plate away without tasting the bread and jam. "I think, nephew, that you had best tell me what this is all about."

He listened to Lord Worth's story without interruption, then sat in thought a moment before he asked, "If you are innocent, why did you run?"

"You don't believe me, then." The words were bitter.

"Oh, I believe you. But I am thinking the way the police, and the world, will think."

"I know. It does look bad. But it all happened too fast for thought. There were two of them and two of us, so we—disposed of them—and I took to my heels.

"But at least I have bought myself some time to discover what really happened. Dibdin believes I shot him, remember? God knows who it was he actually saw. But knowing him as well as I do, he'll stick to his story. He hasn't enough mind to change.

"So how about it, sir? Can I hide out here? I think it unlikely I'll be discovered. They will assume I've left the country. But if I am, you can

25

plead ignorance. I would not, for the world, make you an accomplice."

"I am not concerned with that. I am concerned with you playing detective, though. You can stay as long as you go no farther than the theater and this house."

"Dash it, that's like being under arrest."

"Exactly."

"But how am I going to prove my innocence?"

"You'll leave that up to me."

The discussion was closed. The clown rose and walked very softly to the bedchamber door. With a swift movement he jerked it open.

Miss Persey McCall fell inside.

Chapter Four

LADY LAVINIA HAD CALLED AN EMERGENCY MEETING of the Pickering Club. Her library was not overcrowded, for the club's enrollment was only four and the youngest of their number was now on her honeymoon. Though there were plans for expansion, no females among their present acquaintanceship were deemed worthy of such high honor.

On this particular morning the members were seated at a Pembroke table in the book-lined, oak-paneled room, sipping tea from Sévres cups. The club president was having difficulty getting to the business at hand. For the two other members were full of the news they had gleaned on their way to Grosvenor Street. The town was, they informed their leader, abuzz with it.

"And to think we were observing him in the theater just before it all happened." Adelaide Oliver shuddered as if the juxtaposition had somehow triggered the tragedy.

"Are they certain of the charge?" Lavinia asked. "I can think of nothing more dastardly than shooting someone in the back. I am not personally acquainted with Lord Worth, of course, but I have heard nothing to his discredit."

"Oh, yes, it is quite certain," Jane Abingdon assured her. "Sir Dibdin saw him as he fell. We were told so by Mrs. Randolph. She is a distant relation of the Kirbys, you know."

"Humph." Lady Lavinia disposed of Mrs. Randolph.

"Well, if you do not wish to take her word for it"—Jane was nettled by her friend's attitude—"there were any number of others to tell the exact same story. Sir Dibdin is not in the slightest doubt about his assailant. And the hue and cry is on to apprehend Lord Worth. His associates think they will never catch him, however. They are convinced he has escaped to France."

"That is what his cousin, Mr. Warren, believes," Addie contributed. "He, by the bye, is fortunate to be free himself. The authorities were not best pleased by his part in Lord Worth's escape."

"Fortunate?" Jane's eyebrows rose. "Luck had nothing to say in the matter. I understand it cost his family dearly to buy him off."

"But what a tragedy," Addie sighed. "To think that we were all remarking on what a lovely couple Lord Worth and Miss Hartland made. Now what is to become of her?"

"Oh, I collect she will soon recover," Lady Lavinia prophesied cynically.

"I must disagree," her cousin replied with considerable heat. "Just because you lack sensibility, you think all females are of the same bent. There is such a thing as dying of a broken heart, you know."

"Well, then we shall observe Miss Hartland's decline with interest."

"The thing I cannot understand," Jane interrupted tactfully before the cousins could escalate into a full-fledged quarrel, "is why gentlemen consider dueling a civilized way to settle their disputes."

"Oh, I agree," Addie said. "I, personally, cannot imagine anything more ghastly than being required to stand back to back, then walk ten paces and turn and fire directly at another. It's—it's—barbaric."

"A point of view that Lord Worth evidently agreed with," Lavinia said dryly. "I could admire him if he had simply refused to take part in such an insane ritual. But to shoot an antagonist in the back! That is too cowardly even to contemplate.

"But could we please get to the business at hand?" She rapped her mahogany desk authoritatively with her gavel. "I now declare the meeting of the Pickering Club opened in due form.

"I have convened this meeting for a purpose. The Pickering Club has been given an invitation to perform a service."

Jane and Addie looked at each other uneasily.

"I have here a letter from my brother." She held up the folded missive, with Lord Newbright's seal impressed into the wax, for their inspection. "He requires our presence at Habersham Hall."

"Really?" Addie's face was alight. "How famous!"

Jane was, however, of a more cautious bent. "*Requires?*" she asked.

"Yes, poor George seems to be in quite a taking. You know how reclusive he has become. Well, to be accurate, always was. But while Elinor was alive she dragged him into Society. Well, now it seems he has been maneuvered into giving a house party."

"A house party at Habersham Hall," Addie cooed. "It sounds delightful. I must confess I have been finding the metropolis tedious of late." (The onset of this tediousness had coincided with the departure of Colonel Marston, her particular friend, on a business trip to the north.) "I shall like it above all things."

"Well, Newbright will hate it."

"Then why is he doing it?" Jane was still wary.

"As I was saying, he appears to have been maneuvered into it. It seems that he ran into Colonel Hartland at the Pump Room in Bath a few weeks ago—"

"You surely can't mean the very same Colonel Hartland that we saw at Sadler's Wells?" Addie asked.

"Of course I can. How many Colonel Hartlands do you suppose there are? Now, as I was saying—"

"But what a coincidence!"

"Nothing of the kind. Newbright's quack had prescribed a course of the waters for his rheumatism. And I collect the colonel's physician had a similar notion. It happens with all persons of a certain age. When the doctors know of no other remedy for time's afflictions, they send their credulous patients off to the spas."

"Now, as I recall," Jane reminded her, "you found the mineral waters at Bath quite efficacious."

"Well, yes," their leader conceded, "but I do not think that every ailment—"

Addie, who must have been feeling quite courageous, interrupted once again. "Oh, bother the fusty old waters. The coincidence I was referring to was the fact that Colonel Hartland's name should come up again after we were just discussing him in an entirely different context."

"I repeat. It is not that much of a coincidence. He and Newbright go back for donkey's years. They met at Eton, as I recall. But to get back to the matter at hand, the colonel somehow managed to wangle an invitation to the Hall. Poor Newbright thought he was planning a fortnight of cards. That is my brother's weakness, you know." Her friends nodded. "He can manage to tolerate company at the whist table."

"But only if they keep absolutely quiet during play," Addie added rather huffily while Jane hid a smile.

"Well, er, yes. Anyhow, my brother was quite resigned to the idea. But only, I suspect, because, as usual, he was paying merely half attention to the conversation. Now it appears that it is the theater at the Hall that is the real attraction."

"My goodness," Jane exclaimed, "I had almost forgotten there was a theater."

"As far as my brother is concerned, there might as well not be. It was our grandmother, I believe, who was stage mad and had it built."

"Oh, I remember it well." Addie beamed. "We children used to do some wonderful plays there, remember? *Cinderella* and—"

"*Hansel and Gretel.*" Jane joined in the listing. "You were Gretel, I was the witch and Lavinia was Hansel. She shoved me into the oven, which was actually a trunk upon its side, then latched it and couldn't get me out. I would have smothered if it had not been for the footman."

"And, oh, yes," Addie recalled, "there was the tower she constructed from stacked chairs which collapsed with me when I was Rapunzel and let down my golden hair."

The gavel rapped.

"That is quite enough reminiscing. We have established that there is, indeed, a theater at Habersham Hall. And the colonel intends to make good use of it. He has even bullied Newbright into inviting some professional actors to aid the amateurs. He assures him that the only other thing he need do is provide an audience. In other words, invite his friends and neighbors. Well, needless to say, Newbright is appalled at this turn of events and he wants us to come and take charge."

"Us?" Jane asked. "Don't you mean *you?"*

"No, I do not. He most particularly asked that I bring you two along. He said he hopes to salvage the situation with cards and looked to you, Jane, to partner him." Jane seemed pleased, whereas Addie appeared offended.

"So if there are no objections, we will be leaving in two days' time for the country."

"Does he say whether poor Miss Hartland will be there?" Addie asked.

"She was not mentioned specifically, but I should think she would be among the 'theater loosescrews' that Newbright says will be invading his peace and privacy."

"Then I think it is our duty to go. The poor child must be brokenhearted. Just imagine having one's sweetheart turn out to be a poltroon and a villain. I am sure that we can be a comfort to her. I, especially, am well qualified to bring solace." Tears sprang to her eyes. "I, too, lost the man I loved at an early age."

"For heaven's sake, Addie, there is no similarity

in the two cases. There is no disgrace in dying of the grippe as your Lieutenant Oliver did."

"A broken heart is a broken heart," Addie replied with dignity.

"Oh, very well. I do see what you mean. Now then, do I hear a motion that we remove ourselves in two days' time to Habersham Hall?"

"Oh, for goodness' sakes, Lavinia," Jane protested the formality, "didn't we just say— Oh, never mind." She wilted under the president's frown. "I so move."

"Then I now declare the meeting of the Pickering Club closed in due form."

The gavel banged.

"Ladies, I think the adventure is about to begin."

Chapter
Five

"OH, PERSEY. HOW FORTUITOUS." PICCOLO HELPED
Miss McCall regain her feet. "I was just
about to send for you."

Lord Worth stifled a grin at the actress's embarrassment.

She quickly rallied. "I had expected as much. Indeed, I did not think the interview would last this long. And since I brought him here, I felt responsible."

"Most considerate." The clown's voice was almost
neutral. "Now then. You can take"—he hesitated
for the merest second—"Mr. *Drury* here back to the
theater and familiarize him with the place."

Her chin dropped. "Whatever for?" she blurted
out.

"To keep him from killing himself, primarily. He
needs to know where the traps are, how the machines work. No need to explain to you, surely, all

that a pantomime performer needs to know. Just answer any questions he may have."

"You cannot have engaged him!" She was indignant.

The star looked daggers at the supporting actress. "I hardly see that this is your concern, Miss McCall. But, yes, I have."

"For what, pray tell? An orange vendor?"

Lord Worth shifted uneasily as the two glared at each other. It occurred to him to wonder just what their relation was. It was hard to imagine any ordinary working actor locking horns with the absolute monarch of Sadler's Wells.

"Mr. Drury will be one of our ensemble. He can begin by understudying Harlequin. I suggest that after you familiarize him with the stage trappings, you rehearse the sword fight scene."

"But has he ever played anywhere before?"

"His experience was in Europe," Piccolo snapped. "Not that it is any concern of yours. I am the one who decides such matters. Now, you have wasted enough of my time. Be gone."

"But I can't be saddled with him. I have not yet finished painting scenery."

Piccolo was clearly at the end of his patience. His thunderous look sent her backing toward the door. "The stagehands will finish. Consider this suitable punishment. Now, *go*!

"Oh, by the bye, Mr.—Drury." He opened his door to call after them as the twosome were going down the stairs. "You will be staying here."

"Where?" Miss McCall turned to disagree. "There is not a room to be had."

"He can have Mr. Brooker's till he returns."

"Oh."

Piccolo's bedchamber door slammed and the two young people walked silently out of the house.

They were halfway back to the theater before they broke the silence simultaneously.

"Who is Mr. Brooker?"

"Where in Europe?"

He was first to pick up the cue. "Where in Europe what?"

"Where did you perform?"

"France." He had managed not to hesitate. "Provincial theater."

What a hum! She left the words unspoken, but her look was eloquent enough.

"Mr. Brooker is a member of our company. But he has taken a temporary engagement in Bristol. His specialty is skin work."

"What is that?" He could have kicked himself as soon as the words were out.

"My, you are ignorant, aren't you. He does animal imitations. Uses skins. Must I assume then that the Frogs don't do that sort of thing?"

"You can assume anything you like," he answered shortly, coming to an abrupt halt on the gravel path. "Just tell me one thing, Miss McCall. Why do you resent me so?"

The question was a poser. She could not hope to answer it to his satisfaction. For in all honesty she could not explain it to herself. Any more than she could explain why he had fascinated her so on those two nights when he had sat in the stage box, mesmerized by Piccolo's every move. But she was sure of one thing. He was as bogus as those enchanted castles they erected upon the stage to demolish every night. He was no performer, from France or from the moon. He was a member of the ton. A nob. And why he wished to become a part of the Pantomime defied rational explanation. But that was a minor conundrum compared to the big question: Why had Piccolo, that consummate professional, hired this aristocratic know-nothing?

"Yes?" Worth, who had watched the actress turn all this over in her mind, now prodded. "Just what exactly have I done to set you against me?"

"It is nothing personal," she said stiffly.

"No? You had me fooled."

"It is just that I hate to see an unqualified nob waltz in here and take a position away from a working-class performer."

"Oh, and what makes you think that I am a—nob?"

"Your appearance. Your manner. Your accent."

"Then I must say that it takes one to know one. Your appearance, your manner, your accent, could get you admitted to Almack's."

"But I am an *actress*."

"Well?" His smile said checkmate.

Oh, yes, but I know better. She was not sure just why she left the words unspoken.

The stage area was no longer deserted. A scene painter was completing the job Miss McCall had left unfinished. Carpenters were hammering canvas upon new flats. Stagehands were checking over the machines, making sure that everything was in order for the next performance. All activity came to a halt, however, when Miss McCall entered with a stranger in her wake.

"I would like all of you to meet the newest member of our company," she said formally, with only a slight touch of frost in her tone of voice. "This is Mr. Drury. Piccolo hired him this morning."

"To do what?" The burly carpenter spoke through a mouthful of tacks.

"Piccolo says he'll start by understudying Harlequin."

There was a pause while all hands studied the newcomer.

"Well, then, I'd say 'e's got the legs for it." A rather effeminate little man holding a paintbrush rolled his eyes, and his cronies whooped with laughter.

"Thank you." Worth gave an exaggerated bow, trying not to look as foolish as he felt.

"I'll just show him about a bit. Then Piccolo says we need to work on the sword fight. That is, if there's space." Miss McCall looked doubtfully around the beehive stage.

"Oh, we'll be through here in a tick," the man with the tacks answered her.

"We'll need two catchers, of course." She looked pointedly at the stagehand.

"Glad to oblige," he answered. "You, too, Jackie." He addressed the nearest carpenter, who was large and muscular like himself.

Catcher? Worth wondered, but kept his ignorance to himself. He didn't wish to make another gaffe like skin work.

The tour began with an inspection of the hinged flats that two of the carpenters were working on. "I'm sure you have the same sort of effect in France." Persey McCall's tongue was in her cheek. "So as you know, the point of the thing is that when Harlequin needs to work a miracle, he merely taps his wand and *voilà!* as you Frenchies would say."

With a flourish she pantomimed a magic wand striking the depicted portion of a painted castle. As the "wand" made contact, the top half of the flat fell with a smart crack, transforming the castle into a barred prison.

"Very effective" was Worth's admiring comment.

The carpenters looked pleased. "When we get the whole business lashed together, the audience will think they're seeing a bleedin' miracle, no mistake."

"Now that you know what is coming, you will remember to stand clear, I trust." Miss McCall might have been addressing a three-year-old. "It would rather spoil the effect for Harlequin to get conked upon the noggin."

"I'll keep that in mind."

"And you had better familiarize yourself with the stage traps." She traversed the boards with him, pointing out those places where the floor had been rigged to open downward to allow the arrival and departure of ghosts, demons, and other theatrical institutions. It would not be the thing for you to disappear down hell-mouth. Accidentally."

"Your concern is touching."

"I am merely thinking of the integrity of the Pantomime."

"Why does that not surprise me?" he muttered.

The next stop on the tour was the wardrobe room, where he met the mistress of the robes and marveled at the multitude of costumes required for the Pantomime. The mistress, though ancient, was not too old to be beyond appreciating a handsome young man. Gesturing toward the well-supplied dressing table that also fell within her province, she volunteered to teach him how to apply the Harlequin makeup. Worth took time to thank her courteously even though Miss McCall was waiting impatiently to lead him on to the property room, where all the Pantomime tricks and comic "changes" were stored. "Choose your weapon, sir." She pointed to a large assortment of swords.

All in all, the tour had lasted only thirty minutes. But when they arrived back on the stage, it had been transformed. The scenery was in place for the evening's performance. The paint pails, the cloths, the debris, had all been cleared. But to Worth's dismay, not a stagehand had left. They were all standing around expectantly, waiting for him to go through his paces.

"Here's what we do," Miss McCall instructed. "We start the battle upstage. You drive me, furiously, down to the floats. That is to say, those gaslights there between us and the audience."

"I know what they are." His stare was frosty.

"My mistake. I thought they might be called 'frogs' in France.

"But as I was saying, we fight toe to toe for about a minute. After that, I begin to drive you upstage left. When it becomes apparent to the audience that you are done for, you drop your sword, do a series of handsprings toward the window, then dive headfirst through it. Matt and Jackie will be in place to catch you."

At least that cleared up one mystery. He now knew what a catcher was.

"You fellows get in place. Don't forget your carpet," she called, and the stagehands obligingly moved offstage.

"Now then, do you think you can manage all of that?"

"I believe so. Another question is, do you know how to handle that sword?"

"Oh, I wouldn't worry too much about that." She gave him an evil grin as they took their places in front of the painted backdrop. "En garde!" she shouted, then attacked.

Even with the warning, the ferocity of her onslaught was totally unexpected. It was all Worth could do to defend himself. Never mind the fact that the edges of the swords were blunted, he had no desire to be thwacked with every ounce of strength that this fiery little wench could muster. What was it that Piccolo had said about pantomimists learning their craft as soon as they could walk? Well, the Fury before him must have toddled on-stage with a miniature sword in hand. She definitely knew what she was doing.

"I thought I was supposed to drive you to the floats," he said between clenched teeth, his back pressed against the painted castle wall.

"Only if you're man enough," she taunted.

"I'm man enough to do it," he growled back, parrying a thrust that might have skewered him in a real sword fight. "But I am also gentleman enough not to wish to hurt a lady."

"Oh, there's little chance of that. Have you ever had a sword in your hand before? The French, no doubt, were interested in other things."

That did it. "Defend yourself, Boadicea."

She did. And quite effectively. The ring of stage-hands stamped and cheered as the battle grew more furious. Out of the corner of his eye Worth saw Piccolo watching intently from the wings.

Little by little he forced her downstage toward the floats. Though she tried to make it appear that she was only following the plan she had choreographed, it was obvious to all that she was well and truly beaten.

After they had fought on for several seconds, he gave her a taunting smile. "Now then. At this point I believe I'm expected to let you get the better of me."

"Begin backing up," she said between her teeth,

41

trying not to gasp for breath. "At midstage drop your sword, turn, and run; then dive out the window."

"Run?" His sword flashed through her guard and pricked her lightly in the midriff. "Beg pardon," he grinned. "I did not mean to do that. I *run* upstage? I thought you said I was supposed to do handsprings."

"If you are up to it."

"One can but try."

The tide of battle turned. The "villain" was beating Harlequin steadily stage left. An exaggerated gesture that convulsed the stagehands indicated that it was "bellows to mend" with Mr. Drury. With a piteous groan he threw down his sword. Then in a lightning-swift series of twirls, taken *sans* hands, he landed in front of the upstage window. After sending a speaking look over his shoulder, he dived, headfirst, through it.

And landed with a sickening thud.

Worth lay motionless for several moments, all the breath knocked from his body, wondering if this was what it felt like to die. At last he was able, cautiously, to raise his head and look into the grinning faces of his "catchers."

"Sorry about that, guv." Big Matt struggled, unsuccessfully, to look contrite. "Afraid we stood back a bit too far. Mr. Tessatore, our usual Harlequin, always covers a bit more distance, you see."

Lord Worth was struggling slowly to his feet, ascertaining that except for having had the wind knocked out of him and seeing red, the damage to his body seemed minimal.

But the damage to his pride—that was another matter. This had been, after all, the worst day of his existence. Since sunup, he had sunk from being one of London's most sought-after Corinthians to becoming a disgraced, nameless fugitive from the law. But somehow all that seemed minor compared to this indignity: He, Jonathan Forsythe, the fifth Viscount Worth, had been bamboozled for the entertainment of a group of second-rate thespians. The fact that he might have been maimed for life had only added to the fun. One pretty, laughing face in particular inflamed him. But since there was nothing that he, a gentleman, could do about her, he chose another target and sprang toward it.

The facer that he landed with a lightning left cracked against the stagehand's jaw. The man's eyes glazed, his knees buckled, and he hit the floor like a felled oak. Worth wheeled to attend to the other catcher, but Jackie, no one's fool, had taken to his heels amid the shouts of laughter of his colleagues.

Through a red haze Worth saw his uncle step in front of him to clap a detaining hand upon his shoulder. "Now then, Mr. Drury"—Piccolo spoke heartily—"I see you have been well and truly initiated into our little group of players. Welcome, sir, to Sadler's Wells."

Chapter Six

LORD WORTH MADE HIS STAGE DEBUT THE FOLLOWING evening. He was not ecstatic over his assigned part. He played the vegetable man. His costume consisted of a cabbage body, carrot arms, potato feet, and a pumpkin head crowned with a celery-stalk topknot. And his role in the pantomime plot (if their stage antics could be given such a literary term) was to be the victim of one of Piccolo's famed transformations.

As the scene was sketched, a handsome actor would be in hot pursuit of Columbine. For a while the actress would put up a token amount of coy resistance. But just as her guard was going down and she was about to grant the sought-after kiss, Piccolo, with the aid of some obscuring smoke and a stage trapdoor, was supposed to change his rival into a veritable salad.

As Worth stalked around backstage trying to get

accustomed to the cumbersome costume, his wounded dignity found a target for the resentment that had been building within him ever since the company's makeup artist had turned him into a rabbit's banquet. Columbine flounced past him to take up her position onstage and flashed him an impish grin. He had no further doubt that she was responsible for his casting. He longed to throttle the scheming little minx.

Worth watched through triangle eyes as she joined the dancers stretching onstage, preparatory to the opening number. He had to admit, grudgingly, that she was a stunning-looking Columbine, with her ringlets crowned by a coronet of roses and her low-cut off-shoulder gown showing, in his opinion, far too much creamy skin. Her bodice came to a V at the waistline, emphasizing her shapeliness. The full skirt was made of some gauzy spangled material, ending at her calves. Satin slippers were secured by ribbons round a pair of shapely ankles that made Worth fantasize—

This unproductive reverie was cut short by a clap upon his cabbage shoulder. "Well, you wanted anonymity, did you not?" his uncle said in a low, amused voice. "Your closest friends would never recognize you."

Piccolo strode onstage, the curtain rose, the clown somersaulted down to the floats. "How are you tomorrow?" he joyfully inquired. Once more the performers whirled into their dance, and the magic began.

Worth stood in the wings studying his uncle's antics like an apprentice alchemist convinced that he, too, could find the formula for gold by combining the proper elements. The ingredient that presently absorbed his attention was Piccolo's comic timing.

A second more and the moment would have been lost. A second less and the audience would have been cheated of reaction time. It was during these reflections that his eyes wandered to the boxes. A shock ran all the way through him from pumpkin to potato. For that very same stage box in which he had so recently sat, a carefree man, was now occupied by the same party, *sans* himself, of course.

His first instinct was not to go onstage. Then the absurdity of such a reaction hit him. As Piccolo had said, not even his closest acquaintance— He edged around the concealing scenery to get a better view.

His eyes narrowed behind the pumpkin mask. His "closest acquaintances" seemed to be doing quite well without him, thank you. He watched Miss Pamela Hartland clap her hands delightedly at some outrageous bit of onstage business while his cousin Clarence leaned close to whisper in her ear. If the pair was devastated by his disgrace and flight, they were effectively hiding it.

He had always suspected that his cousin had a tendre for Miss Hartland. He supposed he should not blame him for taking advantage of the circumstances. Still, loyalty was a virtue he had always—

"Bravo!" Colonel Hartland's shout of delight snapped him back to reality. It was almost time to make his entrance. He turned and lumbered down the iron staircase to the lower level, where the stagehands waited to whisk him up through the trapdoor and onto the stage.

The transformation of pursuing lover into vegetable man was greeted by shrieks of amazement and delight from the packed audience. And onstage the action grew even more frenetic. At first Columbine threw up her hands in horror at the change, but she was soon convulsed with traitorous laughter.

Piccolo, delighted with his successful magic, jumped up and down in ecstasy. So did the monkey that the clown had been leading by a chain fastened to his waist.

The monkey was in reality a small child, an example of the "skin work" that Persey had alluded to. As the clown's delight in the transformation increased, he began to turn rapidly in circles, while the little hairy figure ran as fast as its short legs would carry it on the outstretched chain.

But the task soon proved too much for the tiny beast, and to the audience's delight, its feet soon left the stage and the little creature—shrieking its monkey shrieks—was twirled in dizzying circles at the end of Piccolo's chain. The pace increased. The audience screamed with laughter. The little beast was turning in serpentine gyrations, sometimes so low as to skim the stage boards, sometimes so high as to be well above the head of the grinning clown. And it was on one of these high flights that the chain snapped in two.

It all happened too quickly for thought. The audience gasped. The monkey screamed. And the vegetable man leaped high into the air. Even without the encumbrance of his costume, the feat would have been impressive. With it, it seemed impossible. But somehow Worth managed to overcome both the confining bulk and the law of gravity to pluck the little creature out of the air as he went hurtling toward the pit. In the act of rescue, monkey and pumpkin head collided and the latter was sent rolling across the stage.

Columbine unfroze, then quickly reacted. "My hero!" she screeched, and ran to fling her arms around Vegetable Man and monkey. "Duck your head," she whispered to Worth as the monkey wrig-

47

gled free and went howling offstage into his mother's arms. Then to make absolutely sure that the vegetable man's identity not be revealed, Columbine raised herself on tiptoe and kissed him.

It was an aggressive onslaught. Not only did she manage to hide his face with hers, but her arms were thrown around his neck and her hands became entwined in his near-white hair, managing to conceal the most of it. And in her passion she forced the vegetable man backward while the audience, now convinced that the whole thing, including the snapped chain, was a part of the stage business, howled in delight. Meanwhile Piccolo snarled and grimaced in clownish rage, mock-furious that his wonderful transformation had gone awry and the vegetable man had, after all, won Columbine.

The pair was well offstage before the kiss concluded. And it was another lengthy moment before the carrot arms released Columbine. But she still remained pressed, trembling, against a cabbage chest for several seconds—a reaction which she later blamed entirely upon the terror of seeing little Jocko Mullinax go flying through the air to certain death.

Chapter Seven

"**M**R. DRURY" FOUND HIMSELF AN INSTANT HERO. As soon as the curtain lowered for the final time, the common dressing room, where he had gone to remove his vegetation, was invaded by the cast and crew, all eager to shake his hand or to hug him, depending upon the gender of the admirer.

Big Matt, his "catcher," was particularly moved, for he was, as it turned out, Jocko's father. There were tears in his eyes as he pumped Worth's hand up and down long enough to have filled a water trough or two while he mumbled his thanks. "I 'opes there's no 'ard feelings about that other business," he concluded, not quite able to meet Worth's eyes.

"None at all," Worth reassured him. "In your place, I'd have done the same to any green 'un."

When Miss McCall, still in her Columbine costume, approached him, everyone else had drifted away. "That was a fine thing you did," she said. The compliment seemed to cost her.

"Oh, come now. Not you, too." Worth had found all that adulation painfully embarrassing. "It's what anyone would have done when a child came hurtling toward him, for God's sake."

"He didn't come toward you. You had to run for him and leap. And if you hadn't succeeded—" She choked, and her words trailed off.

"Well"—he shrugged—"maybe all those hours on the cricket field weren't entirely a waste of time."

"Oh, they play cricket in France, do they?" she retorted, and he could have kicked himself for the slip-up.

"I did grow up in England, as a matter of fact," he answered.

Yes, I'll wager you did, she answered silently. But aloud she said, "Well, I didn't come here to discuss your background. I did think, however, that I should explain why I—ended the scene the way that I did."

"Oh?" He looked down at her with folded arms. "Are you trying to tell me that you did not have a sudden, irresistible urge to throw yourself into my arms and kiss me? How lowering."

"I thought that you might think exactly that," she scowled, "and I wished to set the matter straight."

"Most thoughtful of you."

"The fact of the matter is, there was your pumpkin head rolling across the stage, and with that white hair of yours—"

"The term is 'blond,' I believe," he interrupted. "That is, unless it has turned white tonight with shock. No, by George"—he had stooped to look into the dressing table glass—"it is still the same."

"The only point about your hair is that it would have become immediately apparent that you were not the original dark-haired Harlequin. So I had to hide you or the effect would have been entirely ruined." She made no mention of his acquaintances in the stage box or of the sixth sense that had told her he would not wish them to know his identity. "And *that* was the only thing I could think of," she ended rather lamely.

"Oh, it was a stroke of genius. Quick thinking and all of that. Much more convincing than wrapping a shawl about my head."

"I did not have a shawl."

"How fortunate for me," he grinned. "I'm sure in that case I should have been smothered."

"Well, as long as there is no misunderstanding."

"None at all. I am keenly aware that you acted in the best interests of the Pantomime."

"She did indeed." Piccolo spoke from the doorway. "That was very quick thinking, my dear. You saved our show from ruin. Illusion is our lifeblood. And once that becomes destroyed, the Pantomime ceases to exist. Now that I think on it," he mused, "I collect we should keep that ending in the scene."

Worth stared at the clown in disbelief. "Surely you are not considering flinging that little beggar—"

"No, no. Of course not. I mean the other bit, where Piccolo does not succeed in vanquishing his rival. After all, the clown needs to be a loser, or how else could so many people identify with him?

"But now let's all go home and get some sleep. I need to talk to you tomorrow, Mr. Drury. In my room. Half past ten. I'll have breakfast sent up for us."

* * *

Worth slept very little that night, and when he did, it was to dream of Colonel Hartland in the stage box hurling a never-ending supply of babies onto the stage which he was forced to catch while iron shackles chained him to the floor. It added insult to injury the following morning to find his uncle looking fresh and dapper in his brocade dressing gown.

"Ah." The clear gray eyes seemed to miss nothing of his nephew's haggardness as they looked him up and down. "I see that the new clothes fit you, more or less."

Worth was wearing a soft, loose-fitting shirt tucked into yellow nankeen trousers. "Yes, thank you for them. And for the room. I am deeply in your debt, sir. I hope to be able to repay you in time."

"You repaid me last night." The clown's face darkened. "Believe me, the person whose job it was to check that chain will live to regret the oversight.

"But as for the clothes, you could not go on indefinitely wearing what you had on your back when you left home. The garments I purchased are a far cry from those you are accustomed to. But Bond Street does not suit your present station. Still, as you no doubt surmised, I have not asked you here to discuss your wardrobe.

"Tell me"—Piccolo was pouring tea—"are you acquainted with a Lord Newbright? His estate is in Berkshire."

"No, actually. Though I do have a nodding acquaintance with his son. With one of his sons, I should say, who is also a member of White's."

"But Lord Newbright would not know you by sight?"

"Is there some reason that he should, sir?"

"Quite the contrary. I have had a letter from him,

you see, requesting a pair of performers to be guests at a house party he is hosting. It seems there is a theater at Habersham Hall, and some of the visiting nobs want to do theatricals. He should like professional assistance, he says."

"But I can't go away," Worth objected. "I need to find out who shot Dibdin."

"I told you I would see to that investigation." Piccolo spoke impatiently. "After last night's episode, it has become clear that you are not safe here. If it had not been for Persey's quick action when you, er, lost your head"—he grinned sardonically—"your identity would have been discovered and you would most likely be cooling your heels in Newgate at this moment. No, Berkshire seems like a good place for you till the hue and cry dies down. That is, if you can continue to be plain Mr. Darcy while you are there. Are you likely to have acquaintances among his guests?"

"I shouldn't think so. He is rather elderly."

"Well, it's settled, then. You and Persey will leave in three days' time."

"Miss McCall is going?" Lord Worth was of two minds about that news.

"Yes. The 'Young Columbine' was invited most specifically. His lordship writes that his guests request her presence." He smiled wryly. "Which is another reason I want you along. To look after her."

"It appears to me," his nephew replied bluntly, "that if some old lecher has his eye on her, you would be better advised to keep her here."

"Unfortunately, we players cannot afford to offend the nobility. We depend upon their goodwill and patronage. Besides, Persey is the only member of my cast who could blend comfortably into such company. With the exception of yourself, of course.

She has had the best of female education. I saw to that."

"*You*, sir?"

"Yes, I. But if you are thinking that Persey is your cousin"—he seemed to stare right through the younger man—"rid yourself of the notion. No, on second consideration, do nothing of the kind. For I would like you to treat her as though she were your blood relation."

"I see."

That was a flagrant lie. He did nothing of the kind. Back in his bedchamber he could not keep the subject off his mind. He certainly had not failed to notice that his uncle demonstrated a proprietary attitude toward the young actress that was not present in his behavior to the rest of the company. And if that attitude was not paternal—well, that left only one alternative.

Lord Worth picked up a pair of donated worked slippers from beside his bed and threw them into the open clothes press with rather more force than a tidying impulse called for.

Chapter Eight

THE OUTSTANDING THING ABOUT THE PICKERING Club's journey to Habersham Hall was that there was nothing outstanding about it. Much to Addie and Jane's relief, the ladies made the trip in Lavinia's well-sprung coach. Each had confessed to the other the fear that once again Lavinia would seize upon some less conventional mode of transportation. A Gypsy wagon perhaps. Or the public coach. They were not even required to wear the club uniform, designed by the president and loathed by the rank and file, consisting of a tentlike tunic billowing over harem trousers.

"Even Lavinia would not upset her brother to that degree," Adelaide had theorized.

"Don't be a sapskull. Since when has Lavinia given a thought to Newbright's—or anyone else's—sensibilities. No, she clearly has something preying on her mind to the exclusion of all else. And you know what that can mean."

The conversation had taken place at the Green Man Inn, where they had stopped for a change of horses. Lady Lavinia, to the ill-concealed disgust of her coachman, was inspecting, and twice rejecting, the teams of cattle which the hostler was attempting to foist upon them. The two ladies who had spent the first part of the journey rejoicing in their good fortune spent the last several miles watching their leader uneasily, trying unsuccessfully to come up with a reason for her faraway look and unnatural quiet.

The coach turned through griffin-topped stone pillars and traversed two miles of driveway winding through a concealing wood before it emerged into an open vista designed by Capability Brown. The ladies were far too familiar with Habersham Hall, built in the seventeenth century after the fashion of Inigo Jones, to be impressed by the imposing edifice that dominated the rise before them. All their attention was focused upon the couple strolling tête-à-tête by the ornamental lake that fronted the mansion. Lady Lavinia was heard to murmur "Ahhh" as if the sight were totally expected.

"Surely that is not Miss Hartland?" Addie exclaimed.

"Oh, but it surely is," Jane assured her. "She does not exactly appear prostrate with grief, does she?" They watched the young lady accept a rose that the young man paused to pluck for her and tuck it into the pink satin ribbon that encircled the waist of her muslin walking dress. "Who is that fellow, anyhow? He looks vaguely familiar."

"He should," Lavinia answered. "He was the other gentleman in the Hartland box at Sadler's Wells."

The ladies were met at the porticoed entrance by Lord Newbright himself, who appeared almost pathetically glad to see them.

There was little resemblance between the brother and sister. Whereas Lady Lavinia's features were sharply defined—indeed, almost hawklike—his lordship's were less memorable. His eyes were pale, his gray hair was thinning, his jawline had slipped into jowls. And while his sister was a lady of action, he was bookish to a fault, an avid student of entomology, particularly butterflies. It was alarming to the three ladies to find his lordship, whose normal facial expressions ranged from bland to preoccupied, now looking quite distraught.

"Vinny, you will have to take over for me here" was his initial greeting as he handed his sister from the coach. "I tell you I'm at me wit's end."

"So it would appear, George. It is quite customary, you know, to greet new arrivals and inquire about their health and the rigors of their journey. And pray do not call me Vinny. You know I hate it above all things."

He waved the civilities away. "That lobcock Hartland can talk of nothing but the Pantomime. The *Pantomime*, mind you. Rope dancing. Fire eating. Juggling. All that sort of thing, for heaven's sake. When I let him talk me into this nonsense, I thought he meant to do Shakespeare—Sheridan— something of that kind. Which would have been bad enough. But the Pantomime! And he insisted that I invite some performers from Sadler's Wells. Should be here anytime. God knows what they'll be like." He shuddered. "Will most likely eat with their fingers."

"Well, it is not like you to notice if they do." His sister spoke soothingly. For her.

"And he wants me to invite the whole county to the performance. The neighbors will think I've taken leave of me senses. Become a complete Bedlamite. Will you please tell me, Vinny, just which of our sapskulled ancestors it was who built that benighted theater? And then explain why someone did not have the common sense to turn it into a conservatory years ago?"

"Never mind, George. And pray do not call me Vinny." They were ascending the marble steps that led to the front entrance. "Now that I am here, I shall assume charge of the production."

"Oh, but I do not think Colonel Hartland will stand for that."

Jane, behind them, smothered a giggle. "Good luck to the colonel," she whispered to Addie.

"The idea was for him to direct the curst production as well as to perform in it. All very well if he'd just get on with the thing and stop badgering me. But it's 'We will need so-and-so, Newbright.' Or 'Could the footman do so-and-so?' He even wants permission to raid me attics for costumes and scenery. Should have stayed in the army, where giving orders and having people jump is the expected thing. Though come to think on it, he was a blasted nuisance even in school. I can tell you now, Vinny, the servants don't like any of it above half."

The out-of-character effusive greeting of his lordship's majordomo appeared to underscore his words. The ramrod-straight butler seemed, figuratively, to unbend. His usually dour expression was all smiles. "His lordship has been looking forward to your visit, ma'am," he said, and the inference seemed to be that so was he as he directed the disposal of the ladies' baggage.

Later, when they were being refreshed by tea in

58

an enormous withdrawing room whose silk wall hangings, ceiling ornamentation, furniture upholstery, and massive picture frames were all of gold while the ceiling, woodwork, and marble fireplace were a gleaming, contrasting white, Lavinia picked up the conversation where her brother had left off. "So am I to understand, George, that you wish me to take over your hostly duties?"

"Want you to do whatever a wife would do in these circumstances."

"I have not the slightest notion of how one might accomplish that. For if I remember your Elinor, she would have stayed in town or on the Continent and not got herself involved. But if you give me carte blanche to do so, I will take charge here. And you can go chase your butterflies in solitude till the place is rid of guests."

"Oh, I couldn't funk the thing entirely." He absentmindedly held out his cup which Jane obligingly refilled for him from the ornate silver teapot left, along with a generous supply of cakes, upon the small table ringed by their chairs. "Not quite the thing, and all that. And I don't really mind playing the host at mealtime. Port and cigars afterward. That sort of thing. In fact, I wouldn't mind a bit of cards before bedtime. Would that suit you, Jane?" For the first time, he seemed to become aware of his sister's friends.

"Indeed, I should enjoy playing whist." Jane smiled and he brightened considerably.

"And, er, you, too, of course, Adelaide," he added politely but with rather less enthusiasm.

"Oh, yes. I quite look forward to cards." Addie's false eagerness to engage in a pursuit that she found trying in the extreme rang just as hollow as his invitation.

The trio's first contact with the other house guests came at dinner, which Lord Newbright insisted upon having served unfashionably early at five. "We keep country hours," he had informed the ladies.

"Knowing your abhorrence of change of any kind, Newbright, I am not surprised," his sister had sighed as they rushed off to complete their toilettes in time.

But she was all amiability as she took her place at the end of the highly polished mahogany table that had been robbed of enough of its leaves to make general conversation possible. She had already thought of several subtle ways of introducing the subject of the Pantomime. But such maneuvering proved unnecessary. Indeed, it would have been impossible to induce the colonel to talk of anything else.

"I think your brother is rather shocked that I chose this particular type of entertainment," he confided to her in a booming voice. "Thought we would go in for legitimate theater stuff. The Bard or some such thing that would bore us half to death. But what Newbright—and most people, come to that—don't understand is that the Pantomime is a genuine art form. We got it from the Frenchies, who copied the Italians. The old commedia dell'arte, as it was known, goes back all the way to God knows when. I do know that the characters were well established by the seventeenth century. They had Arlecchino—he is our Harlequin. There was Pulcinello—we call him Punch—and Pedrolino—our Pierrot. And of course there was the beautiful, naughty Columbina—Columbine, that is—whom they all pursued. Actually very little but the names have been changed down through the years. The characters remain as outrageous as they ever were. Have any of you ever attended the Pantomime?" He enlarged the conversation. "I'll wager all of you went as children."

"As a matter of fact," Addie offered, "it is my most favorite thing. I much prefer it over the theater or the opera." This declaration earned her such a beam of approval that she blushed, then went on to say, "In fact, Lady Lavinia and Mrs. Abingdon here, knowing my partiality, took me to Sadler's Wells recently for a birthday treat."

"Then you saw Piccolo at work." The colonel was delighted. "As a serious student of the art form, I can tell you that his clown has never seen an equal."

"I collect we attended on an evening when you were there," Lady Lavinia said with a studied nonchalance that caused her friend Jane to brace herself. "Let me see. Why, it was only a week ago, actually. On a Saturday evening. Did you not occupy one of the stage boxes?"

"Most probably." The colonel's enthusiasm seemed to be waning. "I attend so often that it is difficult for me to pinpoint an evening."

"Oh, I am certain now it was you that we observed, along with your lovely daughter." Lavinia gave a gracious nod Miss Hartland's way and the beauty lowered her eyes modestly at the compliment. "And why, yes, you, too, were in attendance, were you not, Mr. Warren?" That gentleman looked up from his pheasant and nodded. "And there was another young gentleman with you, was there not, sir?"

The question fell like a stone in the middle of the table.

"I believe Lord Worth was in attendance that particular evening." The colonel might have been making the admission under torture.

"Lord Worth!" Lavinia's surprise should have

earned her center stage at Covent Garden Theatre. "Not that same Lord Worth who shot poor Sir Dibdin Kirby!"

"There could hardly be more than one," the colonel pointed out repressively.

"Eh? What's all this?" Lord Newbright had been evidencing his usual lack of interest in the dinner conversation, but now he was all ears. "What the deuce are you going on about, Vinny? Who shot whom? Whereabouts? And why?"

The other reactions around the table were varied. Jane had watched with detached interest as her friend threw the cat among the pigeons. But as Addie observed the red splotches appear on Miss Hartland's pale cheeks, she looked ready to sink with mortification. Mr. Warren, too, was all concern for the distressed lady. He reached over as if to take her hand, then apparently thought better of the impulse. The colonel outdid the rest by looking thunderous.

Only Lady Lavinia seemed oblivious of the consequences of her probing. "Really, Newbright," she said, "do you never know what is going on in the world? Berkshire is not Timbuktu. People do go back and forth from here to the metropolis. And London Society has talked of little else."

"Has talked of *what*?" Lord Newbright was fast growing exasperated. "Who shot whom, blast it, Vinny?"

"*Do not* call me Vinny. And had you been attending, you would have heard me say that Lord Worth shot Sir Dibdin Kirby." She paused dramatically. "In the back."

"My God!"

"That does rather sum the business up."

"But that's impossible. Don't know the present Lord Worth. Young cove, no doubt. But I know the

62

family. And the Forsythes don't go about shooting people in the back. Never have done. No reason they should start now."

"Oh, I do agree. It does seem improbable. But it appears that there is no doubt in the matter. The victim, you see, positively identified him."

"You mean that Dibdin cove's alive?"

His sister nodded.

"Then that's another peculiar thing. Any Forsythe I ever knew wouldn't of botched the job. If they drew a bead at a cove, that ended the matter. Regular dead-eyes. Every man jack of 'em." His lordship shook his head sadly at the way the House of Forsythe appeared to be declining. "But you ain't said why he shot the fellow in the back, Vinny."

"Do not call me Vinny," she said between clenched teeth. "But to answer your question, it seems there had been some sort of quarrel. Over cards, from what I hear. That is the usual way of it. And a duel had been arranged. Someone informed the authorities, and the police arrived at the scene in time, so they thought, to stop it. But they found poor Sir Dibdin sprawled upon the ground, bleeding. And he identified Lord Worth as his assailant."

"My word!" His lordship was appalled. "But why would he do such a knavish thing?"

"That is easily enough explained." Colonel Hartland's gall had been rising rapidly during the conversation. He now appeared near apoplexy. "The fellow is a coward."

"Oh, come now, sir, I must protest." Mr. Warren was obviously distressed.

"A coward. A dastardly coward." The colonel stuck to his guns. "I realize that this is painful for you, Clarence. Your cousin and all. Still, you might as well face the fact. The man is a coward."

"But there has been nothing in his life heretofore to indicate anything of the kind, sir. Why, my cousin was a regular nonesuch at school. Captain of all the teams. A bruising rider. A champion boxer. Why, there is no sport you can mention in which he did not excel."

"It's natural enough for you to defend him, m'boy." The colonel spoke kindly. "But all that business has nothing to say in the matter. The plain fact was that when he had to face up to a man with pistols at close range, he funked it. Oh, I've seen it happen in battle more than once. Coves under fire—the ones you'd least expect—would turn tail and run. Didn't have the bottom for it. It's the only explanation. The fellow is a coward."

"Really. I do think this subject has gone on far too long."

Everyone, at least everyone who knew Addie well, stared in astonishment. If the soup tureen had interrupted the conversation, it would have been less startling.

"Can you not see that you are distressing poor Miss Hartland? Really, this is most inconsiderate. Now, please do talk of something else. Something pleasant. Flowers, for example."

Lord Newbright, who was slightly hard of hearing, turned to Jane for clarification. "What is it that Addie wishes us to talk about?" he asked in a carrying whisper.

"Flowers. She suggests we talk about flowers."

He looked astounded. "Now, what sort of topic is that, I ask you? What the devil can you say about a bunch of daisies?"

With that he abdicated his hostly duties once again and gave full attention to his mutton.

Chapter Nine

THE TWO SADLER'S WELLS PERFORMERS WERE NOT comfortable traveling companions. They sat side by side in the public coach but found little to say to each other.

Even without the inhibiting presence of the other passengers, Persey would never have shared her thoughts. For the truth was, her mind kept dwelling upon that moment when she had seen the pumpkin head go rolling across the stage and had hurled herself at Mr. Drury like a Covent Garden wanton.

But Columbine *is* a wanton, she defended herself. Her action had not only been resourceful, the embrace had been in character. Moreover, she was a seasoned professional. That was hardly her first stage kiss. And any role that she might play had no effect whatsoever upon her offstage life. So why had she given that particular incident so much as a second thought, let alone kept dwelling upon it like some daft sapskull? A bump in the road jostled her against her traveling companion. She jerked away as though she'd touched hot coals.

"Are you all right?" He had not missed the reaction.

"Yes. No. What I mean is I feel the need for air." She stuck her head out the open window and breathed deeply.

"If you are about to cast up your accounts, let me tell the driver to stop."

The middle-aged couple seated opposite them looked alarmed. "Do you want to face forward, miss?" the husband asked.

"No. No." She smiled wanly. "I'm all right. Really."

Lord Worth, satisfied that her color seemed normal, went back to his own thoughts. They also were not good company. For, according to his uncle's early investigations, his reputation was not just tarnished, it was midnight black. He smiled bitterly as he considered how easily a man's character could be lost. "Fair weather friends." He had never taken time to consider the term before.

Well, no use dwelling on things he could do nothing about. He had best learn more of what was expected of him in the immediate future. Since the couple opposite was now deep in conversation, he took the opportunity to ask his companion, "Have you ever been to one of these country houses before?"

"What's the matter?" she shot back. "Are you afraid I'll dribble the sauce or lick my fingers?"

Gad, she was prickly! He might as well be traveling with a hedgehog. "What I am wondering," he replied with exaggerated patience, "is what exactly is expected of us. Are we guests or the hired help?"

"We are the hired help who will be treated, more or less, like guests."

"Which means?"

"We will eat, sleep, and talk with the gentry, but no one will let us forget that we do not actually belong."

"Oh? I understand that you were asked for particularly. So you must have some acquaintance at Habersham Hall. His lordship, perhaps?"

"No, I have not. Nor do I care for your insinuation. Did it never occur to you that I might have been asked to take charge of these amateur theatricals because I am very good at what I do?"

Well, frankly, no. He was prudent enough not to speak aloud, however. But such a possibility had not occurred. Oh, what she said was true enough. She was an excellent performer. But even more than that, she was a very appealing young woman. Too appealing by half, if you asked him. And why, if his uncle had the kind of relationship with her that he appeared to have, he would allow her to go traipsing off into a possibly compromising situation was past all understanding. True, he himself had been commissioned to keep her out of mischief. But who was supposed to chaperon the chaperon? This line of thought was even more unacceptable than his earlier worries. He took another tack.

"Tell me, why does Piccolo call you Percy?"

"Because it is my name."

"But that's a man's name."

"It isn't P-E-R-C-Y," she said, spelling it out. "It's P-E-R-S-E-Y."

"Don't think I've ever heard that before. A pet name, is it?"

"No. It's a diminutive."

"A diminutive of what?"

"Never mind."

"Persey. Persey. Persey," he mused aloud. Lord Worth, who had spent considerable time in school, choked suddenly. "Oh, surely not!"

Her only answer was a frigid look.

"You surely are not named Persephone?"

More silence.

"The Greek goddess who pops up out of Hades every spring?" His grin widened.

"Well, at least it *is* my christened name," she retorted. "Whereas yours is as false as that pumpkin head you wore. Mr. *Drury* indeed! Piccolo could have been a little less obvious with his inventions. Why didn't he just call you Mr. Covent Garden? Or, for that matter, plain Mr. Lane?"

They finished the remainder of the journey in silence.

They were met in the village by Lord Newbright's crested carriage. As they entered the estate gate and made their way up the long carriage drive, then on to the open vista, if "Mr. Drury" was impressed by the Hall, he did not show it. His companion, on the other hand, was obviously too awed by the Carolean grandeur to keep her vow of sophistication. "How old do you suppose it is?" she asked.

There was no answer. He had suddenly stiffened and was staring with an expression bordering on horror at the two figures seated upon a stone bench beside the lake. The young man held a small volume in his hands and was evidently reading aloud. Persey followed her companion's gaze and had no trouble identifying the beauty of the stage box and the other young gentleman who had been her companion.

"I can't stay here."

"You have to," she protested.

"I said I cannot. It's impossible."

"Because you mustn't meet those people? Well, don't act too hastily. Go on to the stables with the carriage while I scout the lay of the land. Perhaps they are only here for tea."

Whether he liked her plan or not became academic, for the carriage was pulling up in front of the Hall and a regal lady in black bombazine was standing on the steps to greet them. Persey jumped out and hissed at the coachman, "Drive on to the stables immediately. The other passenger is not getting out." The coachman looked surprised but responded to the pretty actress's urgency. He sprang his cattle. Even so, Lady Lavinia, who was now descending the marble steps, caught a glimpse of fair hair and a handsome face under a gray top hat.

"Ah, Miss McCall, is it not?" Her ladyship's smile was cordial, intended to put the young stranger at ease. "I am Lady Lavinia, his lordship's sister. Newbright has delegated me to bid you welcome. But where is your companion? Unless I mistake the matter, we were also expecting an actor from Sadler's Wells."

Persey quickly made up her mind. "Oh, yes, an actor did come with me. But he has gone on to the stables to, er, see to the horses."

If Lady Lavinia found this stranger's concern for his host's cattle peculiar, to say the least, she did not betray it in her expression. "I see," she smiled.

But the lameness of the excuse was not lost upon Persey. She tried again. "The thing is, our Harlequin is quite shy of company. And with good reason," she sighed, warming to her narrative. "He was in a theater fire, you see, and his face became quite hideously scarred."

"How tragic. Especially for a performer," Lady Lavinia murmured.

"Not so tragic for the Pantomime as for other forms of theater. Nor did the fact that the accident also left him mute put a period to his career."

"Well, that is fortunate." If her ladyship's tone was rather dry, it escaped Miss McCall's notice. For the butler had opened the door for them and she was trying not to gawk at the black-and-white marble floor or the intricately carved wooden staircase or the brilliant plasterwork. She especially refused to stare at the ancestral portraits that crowded the walls.

"So you can understand why he will not be joining the company except in the theater. He is painfully self-conscious. I hesitate to ask, but would it be possible to be removed from the other guests? I hope that this will not unduly upset any arrangements." How many bedchambers would this palatial hall contain? The mind boggled. No need to suggest the attic.

"There will be no difficulty in seeing to your Harlequin's privacy. Carson"—Lavinia turned toward the butler—"put our two theatrical guests in the east wing," she ordered, then explained to Persey, "The rest of the party is situated in the other wing. Your colleague's path need not cross theirs unless he chooses it. I take it that your luggage is still in the coach?" She turned again to the butler. "I will show Miss McCall to her chamber myself."

Persey followed her ladyship up the sweep of stairs. "It may seem rather odd that Piccolo chose to send an actor with so many handicaps," she improvised, "but the thing is, Mr. Drury is a Harlequin par excellence. But more important perhaps is the fact that unlike most actors, he is a master of stagecraft."

"And I collect that he also serves as your, ah, protector?" It had occurred to Lady Lavinia that this attractive young person could certainly use one. Whether there was more jeopardy in traveling in a public conveyance or visiting in a country house remained to be seen. Behind her bland hostess face, Lady Lavinia's ever-active mind was outleaping the acrobatic Piccolo himself and arriving at her own conclusions.

"I will leave you now to freshen up," she said politely after she'd ushered the actress into an old-fashioned bedchamber furnished with dark, heavy furniture and decorated with threadbare tapestries. "Dinner is at five. My brother still insists upon country hours. Your luggage should arrive momentarily. If you need anything else, just ring." She nodded toward the bellpull.

"Thank you, Lady Lavinia," Persey smiled. "I think I shall lie down a bit. The journey was rather tiring."

Lady Lavinia shut the door firmly behind her, then hurried to a window in her own bedchamber that overlooked the stable path. She had not long to wait before she spied their resident actress, skirts hiked above her ankles, racing down it.

Chapter Ten

PERSEY WAS SAVED BY LADY LAVINIA FROM HAVING TO repeat her Banbury tale. When she joined the other guests for dinner, Harlequin's absence had already been explained. Nor was he missed. At least Colonel Hartland did not mention the disfigured actor when he swooped down upon her and did his utmost to monopolize her for the evening.

His table conversation was beyond reproach, dealing with the entertainment that he had in mind and deferring to her professional expertise on how best to achieve the desired results. But his melting looks—or leers—were disconcerting and his leg pressed against her own beneath the table offensively.

The first time the contact happened, she assumed it accidental and merely shifted her position. The second time there could be no mistaking his intention. She jerked her leg away, gave him a speaking look, and turned her attention to Mrs. Oliver, on her right.

Lavinia, opposite her brother at one end of the table, was well aware of which way the wind was blowing. She promptly engaged the reluctant colonel in a conversation that kept him occupied throughout the remainder of the meal.

Addie was eager for an opportunity to speak to a star of Sadler's Wells. Actually, she would have been pleased to talk with almost anybody, for Lord Newbright, sandwiched as he was at the head of the table between two unescorted women, still remained his usual taciturn self. Jane had managed to elicit a snippet of conversation, but Addie was too intimidated by the preoccupied peer even to try. So when Miss McCall turned to her with a trite remark about the pleasures of the country, she was overjoyed.

"Oh, Miss McCall," she gushed, "I have been dying to say how much I have enjoyed your performance. The Pantomime is my very favorite thing. So much so that Lady Lavinia and Mrs. Abingdon"—she nodded toward her friends—"took me to Sadler's Wells as a special birthday treat. And I cannot recall when I have enjoyed myself so much."

"I am very glad," Persey smiled. Addie's enthusiasm was totally unexpected in these sophisticated surroundings. She might have been a Cheapside fishwife or a child from anywhere. "Piccolo is marvelous, isn't he?"

"Oh, yes, indeed. But you are, too. I cannot imagine a better Columbine. Oh, I know that Lavinia swears you missed a cue," she said ingenuously, "but I'll not believe it. Your performance was flawless."

"You were there on that particular night?" Persey blurted out before she thought.

Addie's eyes widened. "You mean it really did happen?"

"Well, yes, actually." The professional actress looked embarrassed.

"Pray do not admit it to her ladyship," Addie whispered. "As it is, she is too smug by half."

"But what a strange coincidence." Persey, too, lowered her voice. "How odd that you and your friends and Colonel Hartland and his daughter were all in the audience on that particular night."

"Yes, I know. They were in the box opposite ours. We noticed them in particular."

"And Mr.—Warren, is it?"—Addie nodded—"was also along. But wasn't there another young man in the party?"

Addie looked uncomfortable and darted a quick look across the table. Mr. Warren and Miss Hartland were absorbed with each other. "Yes, there was," she whispered. "It is a terrible tragedy. A scandal. Best not speak of it here."

"Oh" was all Persey could think of to say.

Addie, however, was at no loss for words. She went on to quiz the performer about the various transformations that had taken place onstage and to inquire how they had been achieved. She could hardly wait to impart this specialized information to the other Pickerings. She was certain that Lady Lavinia would insist that it be recorded in the minutes of the club.

Persey was burning with curiosity and thought the meal would never end. When Lady Lavinia at last gave the signal for the ladies to leave the gentlemen to their port, she quickly attached herself to Mrs. Oliver and asked for a word in private. The reason she gave for prying into the other guests' private affairs was that she did not wish to make some dreadful faux pas through ignorance.

Addie was most understanding and led the actress to the empty library. As soon as they were side by side upon a settee, she poured out the tale of the proposed duel and the cowardly attempt at assassination.

Persey's shock was genuine. And afterward her polite conversation in the withdrawing room was pure theatrical technique. For now that she knew the truth about "Mr. Drury," the problem was, what should she do with this terrible knowledge?

The house party broke up early for the evening. As Persey was bidding her host and hostess good night, the colonel bore down upon them. "You must allow me to show you the theater, Miss McCall."

"Can that not wait until morning, Colonel Hartland? I am sure that Miss McCall must be fatigued from her journey." Lady Lavinia's level look might have given a more sensitive individual pause. The colonel was unaffected by it.

"Nonsense. This is the shank of the evening for an actress, is it not, Miss McCall? Why, the curtain has not yet fallen at Sadler's Wells. Besides, I'm sure that you will sleep all the better for knowing exactly what you will be working with."

"Yes, I collect that the sooner I see the stage, the sooner I can plot our action." It was the professional speaking. But the reply had earned her a reproving frown from her hostess until she added, "Will you give me a moment, sir, to go fetch my colleague? He is even more concerned with the stage business than I." Persey hurried off too quickly to see the colonel's crestfallen look or Lady Lavinia's smirk at his discomfort.

Persey was not sure herself why she was rushing toward Mr. Drury's chamber. Should she tell him to leave Habersham Hall this very night? On the other hand, if he desired to stay, there was no time like the present for testing his disguise. If his mask and his muteness kept his identity from the colonel, it should work with the others. Certainly none of his "friends" would expect him to have gone to earth in the Pantomime. (And when it came to that, why he had done so was a mystery to her as well.) So perhaps he could get away with staying here after all. Whether he *should* get away with it was not a moral issue she could struggle with at the moment.

She knocked softly upon his door, then, when there was no answer, more loudly. She tried the knob and the door opened. "Mr. Drury, are you asleep?" She stepped inside. The moonlight streaming across the bed showed it was empty.

Blast! She had told the man to stay in his chamber. Well, perhaps he had bolted. She could hardly blame him. But a glance at the dressing table revealed that his razor and brush were still there. He was simply wandering about, then. Well, on his head be it. Why should she concern herself with a knave who would shoot a gentleman in the back? And how much, if any, of "Drury's" history had Piccolo known? Should she send a message in the morning telling what she had discovered? Then perhaps he could think up some excuse to call her back.

While all these thoughts jumbled through her head, she was walking slowly back toward the main part of the house. She paused a moment to look out a hall window at the moon-bathed view. She was staring down at an old-fashioned formal garden, its geometric pattern outlined in low-cut hedges. She breathed in the scent of roses appreciatively and was just about to turn away when some movement caught the corner of her eye. She looked closer and in the shadow of a large Grecian marble that formed the focal point of the design spied a couple locked in a passionate embrace. The faces were indistinct, but there was no mistaking Miss Hartland's white gown; its silver threads sparkled in the moonlight. Persey had no doubt that Lord Worth's absence was now explained.

That imbecile! she raved silently, not bothering to analyze the stab of jealousy she felt. If he thinks that female is capable of keeping his identity a secret, he certainly is no judge of character.

It occurred to her that she was in no position to criticize. She had certainly misread his lying lordship's character. Well, he could go to perdition in his own fashion. It was no affair of hers.

She was turning away when her eyes swept past and then returned to another figure, standing in the deeper shadows, partly concealed by a rose tree and so motionless that she had almost mistaken it for a statue. In truth, the silver hair did have the gleam of marble. But as she watched, the figure melted back farther into the shadows. The lovers were slowly drawing apart. And the kissing gentleman was Mr. Warren.

Persey was mortified by the relief she felt.

Chapter Eleven

COLONEL HARTLAND WAS NOT OVERJOYED WHEN Lady Lavinia joined them in the theater. But Miss McCall, who had spent more time in dampening the colonel's ardor than in exploring the stage, gave her hostess a grateful look. And when her ladyship volunteered to accompany her to the east wing "just to make sure that Mr. Drury has everything he needs," the colonel, who had intended to see the pretty actress back to her chamber (and with luck, across the threshold), sulkily gave up his pursuit.

"Well now, I do not see any light showing." Lady Lavinia straightened up from squinting at the crack underneath the actor's door. "So I must presume," she whispered, "that he has retired for the night. Do let me know tomorrow whether his meals have been served satisfactorily."

"I will. And I thank you for your concern, your ladyship." There was a double meaning in the actress's expressed gratitude that earned her hostess's approval.

Persey closed the door behind her and leaned against it for a moment while the evening's events whirled like a kaleidoscope before her eyes. Thanks to the garrulous Mrs. Oliver, the mystery of "Mr. Drury's" identity had been solved. The problem facing her now was what to do with the newfound knowledge. She resolutely jerked her mind away from the despicable thing he had done. She was not able to deal with that just yet. In fact, she was not able to deal with anything, she realized as a wave of exhaustion swept over her. She would sleep on it; then perhaps tomorrow she would know what course of action she should take.

She moved away from the door and sank down upon the dressing table bench to remove her slippers. She froze in the act, however, as she heard a rustling noise beneath the large canopied four-poster across the room from her. Her lips were parted for a scream when "Mr. Drury," Harlequin mask in hand, came rolling out from underneath the damask bed hangings.

The scream transformed itself into a stifled "You!"

"Whom were you expecting, Colonel Hartland?" he asked testily as he slapped away the dust a careless chambermaid had missed.

"Hardly." She did not care for the insinuation. "I bade him good night in the theater only minutes ago."

"Well, when I looked in on you earlier, I did not think he would part company so easily. He appeared to have developed at least one more set of hands."

"And did you happen to note that I dodged them all?"

"Yes, to your credit. And you will be well advised to continue to do so. Don't think for one minute that the old lecher's intentions will be honorable. He is notorious for his affairs with actresses."

"Well, thank you for the warning," she said icily, "but I was not born yesterday and he is not the first gentleman to try to seduce me."

"No, I don't suppose he is, but he may be the most practiced. He has, after all, been at it since before you were born."

"Does it not strike you, Mr. *Drury*"—she put an unnecessary emphasis upon his false name—"that this conversation is wide of the mark? We are discussing my affairs, when we should be discussing yours. Now, would you mind telling me just what your connection is with these people and just why you are avoiding them?"

There was a lengthy pause. He sat down upon the bed while a mental struggle appeared to be going on. But finally he answered. "Let's just say that we have been intimates. But I have had serious financial reverses and can no longer maintain my station in society. And"—he waved the Harlequin mask back and forth—"I dislike the idea of their learning that I have come to this."

"I see." She glared daggers. "You are trying to tell me that you wish to conceal the fact that you have sunk so low as to become an actor."

"No need to take offense. Ours is not a classless society, you know."

"And Miss Hartland? Was she an 'intimate'?"

"I believed we were rather more than friends," he admitted.

"Well, she is obviously a friendly person. As Mr.

Warren could testify. Oh, no need to look at me as if I am letting some cat out of the bag. I saw you spying on them in the garden."

"I was not spying. I merely left my room for some air, and they happened along."

"Aren't you the peripatetic one." She was rather proud of her vocabulary. "You managed to look in on everyone. But now the question is, what are you going to do?"

"What do you mean, what am I going to do? That has been decided."

"But you can't remain here."

"Why not? You are the one who convinced me there was no problem. Mute. A disfigured face. A Harlequin mask. No, I shall stay. No one is going to recognize me."

"Oh, no? How do you suppose I recognized you so easily in the garden?"

"I know. I should not have gone out without my mask. But I will remember it from now on," he vowed.

"It was not your face I saw. So if you insist upon remaining, we will need to make some other changes." She had risen and was rummaging through her case of theatrical makeup. "Ah, yes. Here it is." And she held up a small bottle filled with jet black liquid. "This should be the very thing."

"For what?"

He looked from the bottle to the actress with growing apprehension.

Ever since her arrival, Addie had been longing for a private word with Miss Hartland. It was all very well for Lavinia to scoff at the idea of her comforting the beautiful young woman. But while she was prepared to defer to her friend's superiority in most areas, when it came to broken hearts, Lavinia was completely out of her depth. Addie was confident that only a female who had known heartache could understand the problems of another sufferer. And, despite all outward appearances and Mr. Warren, Addie was convinced that Miss Hartland was suffering from just such a malady.

The opportunity arose the next morning. Addie found Miss Hartland alone in the library. The young woman was gazing rather helplessly at the floor-to-ceiling shelves covering three walls. "One hardly knows where to look," she observed when the door closed behind the newcomer.

"I know. Lord Newbright's taste in literature does rather run to butterflies." Addie joined Miss Hartland in her perusal of the shelves and shook her head sadly over the lepidopteran titles. "You are quite welcome to borrow one of my horrid mysteries. I always bring a supply when I come here. I don't know if you enjoy that sort of book, of course." But she looked hopeful.

"Oh, I do indeed." But then Miss Hartland's face fell. "Only Papa does not approve of them. But I thank you for the kind offer in any case."

"But he need not know, need he?" Addie was a bit shocked at herself. It occurred to her that Lavinia's influence might be having a certain corrupting effect, but still— "Under any other circumstance," she hurried to explain, "I would not dream of influencing you against your father's wishes, but no gentleman, no, not even a father, can understand the torment you are experiencing at this moment. I have been longing for a comfortable coze with you, my dear. For you see, I *do* understand."

"You do?" The young woman seemed uncomfortable with the intensity of the sympathy in the large blue eyes. She rather reluctantly allowed herself to be guided to a pair of chairs placed facing the window for an optimum view of the ornamental lake.

Addie leaned toward the other as soon as they were seated. "The thing is," she confided, "I lost my dear husband shortly after we were wed. He, like your father, was a military man—which gives us another bond. So you see, my dear Miss Hartland, I do know the heartache you are going through." She reached to clasp the other's hand. Tears welled in her eyes.

Miss Hartland looked decidedly ill at ease. "You are referring, I collect, to Lord Worth?"

Addie nodded and squeezed her hand.

"But we were not actually betrothed, you know. I should not wish you to refine too much upon our— association."

Addie gave her a shrewd look. "Your father is determined that you forget the unfortunate young man, is he not?"

She nodded.

"But you are finding that impossible. Now, confess it."

The other frowned thoughtfully. "There is no denying that Lord Worth was considered the finest catch in London," she mused. "And he is, quite easily, the handsomest man I know."

"Oh, yes, indeed. When I saw you both at Sadler's Wells, I thought the two of you were the most striking couple I had ever seen. You might have been the prince and princess of some fairy tale."

Miss Hartland blushed modestly.

"Ah, yes," Addie summed up her case, "it was obvious to me that you two were meant for each other. You must not allow your father to keep you apart, my dear. When Lord Worth sends for you, you must go."

The young woman looked taken aback. "What do you mean, when he sends for me? He cannot do that."

"But of course he will." Addie patted the hand she held. "You must simply be patient and bide your time."

"You must not understand properly, Mrs. Oliver. Lord Worth is in disgrace. Papa says that if he ever shows his face again in England, every right-thinking person will send him to Coventry."

"Then you shall have to live abroad."

It would have been obvious to anyone but Addie that Miss Hartland had concluded she was dealing with a Bedlamite. "Leave England? Oh, I could never do that."

"Only long enough to allow the scandal to die down. People do forget, you know."

"Papa says that one must never forget—or forgive—cowardice," the other said primly. "To shoot another gentleman in the back—that is the basest form of cowardice."

"But perhaps there is some explanation." Addie had let go of the young lady's hand. As a romantic heroine, Miss Hartland was beginning to leave a bit to be desired.

"What explanation could there possibly be?"

"Well, how should I know? Perhaps he tripped and the gun went off accidentally."

"I suppose that *could* happen." The young person sounded doubtful.

"Of course it could. You must not allow your faith in Lord Worth to waver. There has to be some logical explanation for his conduct."

"It does seem odd that someone who looks as manly as Lord Worth could turn out to be a coward. Still, Papa says that appearances can be deceiving."

"I do not wish to undermine your father's influence, my dear," Addie pressed her advantage. "But I do feel that love must always have the benefit of the doubt."

They were interrupted by the door opening. "Oh, there you are, Addie." Jane came in, followed by Lord Newbright. "I wondered where you had gotten to. We are going to work on the guest list for the theater evening. I trust we will not disturb you."

"Oh, not at all." Miss Hartland seemed inordinately glad to see them. "I was just leaving. Letters to write, you see."

"Oh, but I wish to show you my collection of horrid mysteries," Addie called as the young person hurried away.

But Miss Hartland must not have heard. The door closed firmly behind her.

Chapter Twelve

F ROM THE VERY FIRST MEETING IN THE THEATER, THE question of who should take full charge of the amateur/professional production was never in any doubt. At least not to those well acquainted with Lady Lavinia. Miss McCall, of course, thought she had been invited for just that purpose. But when her ladyship stated that she would serve best by confining her talents to stage direction, Persey gladly yielded the greater authority.

The colonel was not quite so malleable. He pointed out, very starchily, that (a) he was accustomed to leadership, (b) he was a life-long student of the Pantomime, and (c) the whole thing had been his idea in the first place. Lady Lavinia squelched these arguments with a set-down look and a leveler: She was acting "in loco" Lord Newbright, owner of the theater.

The first order of business was casting. "But that

has already been determined," Colonel Hartland sputtered. "Our professionals will play their Sadler's Wells roles, Harlequin and Columbine, and I shall do the Piccolo parts."

"Perhaps," her ladyship conceded. "But it is only fair to give the rest of the aspirants a chance." She gestured at the members of the house party, the handful of staff she had pressed into service, and a few near neighbors and villagers who had dropped by from curiosity. "Who knows what hidden talent we may uncover." She ignored the colonel's snort.

"Just what do you expect to do about him, pray tell?" Colonel Hartland jerked his thumb toward the stage.

Its lone occupant was a figure, lounging, arms folded, against the back wall, surveying the people milling about in the auditorium through the holes of a black mask.

That mask covered his entire face with the exception of mouth and chin. A bicorne hat crowned his head, concealing most of his hair. The bit that did show was an inky black. He was clad, neck to ankle, in a one-piece diamond-print garment, basically claret colored but with its geometric patterns outlined in silver and in black. The costume hugged his body like a second skin. A small ruff at the neckline and silver buttons marching down the front did little to draw the eye away from an athletic, well-formed male body. The overall effect was to cause some of the more idealized works of long-dead sculptors to come leaping to the mind.

"Hmmm," Lady Lavinia mused. "I see what you mean."

The colonel pressed his point. "He, obviously, has to be Harlequin."

"Obviously."

"Miss McCall tells me that the fellow can't—or won't—remove that mask. So that settles that."

"Oh, the mask is not the problem. His disfigured face could be covered in any number of ways. The vegetable man's pumpkin head, for one example. It is his costume that poses the real problem. I doubt any other male here could fit it quite so— effectively."

"Humph!" the colonel snorted, and pulled in his stomach.

"Now then!" Lady Lavinia raised her voice and thumped the floor with the ebony stick she was carrying. "Shall we get started? If you will all take your seats here in the first two rows, we will begin our auditions. As you can see, our Harlequin has already been cast. He is Mr. Drury of Sadler's Wells."

"Here! Here!" Addie clapped admiringly to her subsequent embarrassment.

"Now then, although Miss McCall, another professional"—she quelled Addie with a look before she could repeat her accolade—"ordinarily plays the part of Columbine, she is so versatile that she can fill in for us in any capacity and will gladly forego the part if anyone else should qualify. Is there anyone here who would like to try for the part of Columbine?" Her eyes scanned the collected group, pretending not to see her cousin Adelaide's hand, which was being timidly raised and then as quickly lowered.

"Well then, Miss McCall, it seems since no one else feels up to the challenge that you—"

"I should like to try." A low but determined voice spoke up. Lavinia turned to find its source. That proved no problem. Everyone was staring at Miss Hartland. Her cheeks had turned a pinkish cast

88

from all the attention, but her expression was determined.

"Oh, come now. I should hardly think—" her father glowered.

"Why not? I have attended the Pantomime with you ever since I was a child. Why, I used to pretend—"

"That is hardly the same thing," her father interrupted, "as disporting yourself upon the stage."

"But is that not why we are here, sir? To disport ourselves upon the stage?"

"Miss Hartland is quite right." Lady Lavinia had had enough of the argument. "As I said, everyone should have an equal chance. Come, my dear." And she gestured toward the stage.

Lavinia stood in the small orchestra pit while the beauty ascended the steps and walked self-consciously onstage. "Why not do the scene, Miss Hartland, when Columbine first meets Harlequin and flirts outrageously with him. He resists at first, but gradually succumbs to her spell. Then, just as it becomes evident that he is well and truly smitten, she reveals herself as a wanton tease, eludes his embrace, and skips from the stage. Do you think you can do that bit of business?"

The young lady nodded. But the look she darted nervously toward Harlequin brought nursery tales of chickens and foxes to Lady Lavinia's mind.

Among the spectators there might have been a contest in progress between the colonel and Mr. Warren as to which could look more disapproving. Mr. Warren at the moment had the edge. Miss McCall, with the advantage of a lifetime spent acting, was busy creating a new role. But her detached observer proved to be wasted effort. Everyone's attention was upon the stage.

Lady Lavinia rapped her cane upon the floor and the buzzing in the auditorium ceased. "All right, Harlequin, shall we begin?"

All eyes were fastened upon him as Harlequin left his leaning position and sauntered down the stage. No one, with the exception of Miss McCall, could have guessed that he was almost as apprehensive and as much a novice in his role as was Miss Hartland. He passed her, in character, with an indifferent nod while still managing to register a clinical appreciation of her beauty.

Columbine's reaction was less than subtle. Miss Hartland's pretty face assumed an exaggerated pout. Her dainty foot stamped the floorboards until they shook. She ran around Harlequin to plant herself squarely in front of him, tilt her head up, close her eyes, and part her lips expectantly. There was a lengthy pause. The mask hid any expression that might be playing upon the actor's face. The body could have been carved in stone. Then, just as Columbine's lashes were beginning to flutter open, he slowly pulled her against his chest and kissed her. Columbine's hands reached up to try to push the two of them apart and then fell weakly to her sides as the kiss intensified.

"That will do!" the colonel barked.

Mr. Warren took a few steps toward the stage and then, with effort, restrained himself.

Lady Lavinia gave the colonel a censorious look for preempting her prerogatives, then echoed his sentiments. "Yes, that is sufficient, thank you. We have seen enough, I collect, to make up our minds."

Columbine and Harlequin drew apart. Her face had gone from pink to fiery red. With demurely lowered eyes she left the stage. Harlequin's retreat to his earlier position revealed nothing of what he might be feeling.

"Now then, Miss McCall, will you enact the same scene, please?" Lady Lavinia smiled toward the actress.

Colonel Hartland seemed hell-bent upon being an obstructionist. "It is hardly necessary for Miss McCall to audition. In fact, if you ask me, the notion smacks of insult."

"Not at all." Miss McCall spoke for herself. "Lady Lavinia is quite right to give everyone an equal chance." She strode purposefully onstage.

This time Harlequin was not allowed to remove himself from his lounging position before the temptress began to entice him out of his indifference. The small audience giggled as the lounging body tensed and the mask turned to watch the swaying hips that sauntered past him. There followed a prolonged game of entice and then retreat as the pretty coquette lured, then turned laughingly away when the more and more smitten Harlequin sought to take her in his arms. Then, finally, when his frustration had reached the point of persuading him to abandon the pursuit, she appeared to succumb and slowly turned to face him, head upturned, lips puckered invitingly, and eyelids fluttering closed. But just as he pantomimed his triumph and reached out to embrace her, she tossed her head and laughed, ducked beneath his outstretched arms, and, accompanied by laughter, scampered off the stage.

No sooner had she reached the wings, however, than two strong arms dressed in motley pulled her, heels dragging, back to center stage. Harlequin then tossed her, whirling high up in the air, caught her, pulled her close, and exacted his kiss while the audience whooped with laughter and applauded.

"I think that will do," Lady Lavinia interrupted dryly when the kiss became prolonged. "We clearly have seen enough to form an opinion."

Chapter
Thirteen

"HAVE YOU ENTIRELY LOST YOUR MIND?" PERSEY fumed. "Just what did you think you were up to?"

Lord Worth had opened the seething actress's door intending to say good night. She had jerked him inside and slammed it behind them. The fury that had been building during the last phase of the tryouts was ready to erupt.

For once Persey had found herself in accord with Colonel Hartland—the Pantomime auditions were a waste of time. For in the end the roles had been cast as he had intended. She would be Columbine (Miss Hartland had voluntarily withdrawn, saying that, after all, she would prefer to sing), Mr. Drury, of course, was Harlequin, and the colonel would play Pantaloon. (To her surprise, he had turned out to be quite good.)

It had taken forever, but finally the other entertainments had been settled on. One of the footmen had a trained dog act; a neighbor played the harp (indifferently, it seemed, but Lord Newbright had let his sister know it was obligatory to ask her). The inclusion of the village Morris dancers was also a diplomatic necessity. But the biggest surprise of the evening came from Lady Lavinia herself, who had declared her intention of engaging in a sword fight. (Here Jane and Addie had gaped at each other.) Of course she would need an adversary. At this point she had looked straight at Harlequin, who, after the slightest hesitation, had nodded his agreement. Satisfied, she had then dismissed the company, detaining only the colonel for consultation upon a point or two. Whether her intention was to smooth his ruffled feathers or to prevent him from following Miss McCall was known only to herself.

Now, inside Persey's bedchamber, Lord Worth removed his black satin mask with a heavy sigh. "Blast! This thing is hot." He twirled it on its ribbons. "Still"—he rubbed the stubble on his cheeks—"the bright side is, there's little need to shave."

"Don't change the subject."

The sigh was deeper this time. "I did not know we had one. Well, that is not precisely true. I have been aware all evening that you are dying to ring a peal over me. But that is hardly a new state of affairs. Do you mind if I make myself comfortable for the tongue-lashing?" He ambled across the room and sprawled upon a couch, resting his crossed ankles upon one cushioned end. "Actually, for the life of me I don't see what has put you into such a taking," he said reasonably. "I was the soul of cooperation, even agreeing to sword-fight with a lady old enough to be my mother."

Persey had followed him and now stood glaring down at his reclining form, arms akimbo. "You did far more than cooperate and you dashed well know it. What did you mean by kissing—Columbine?"

His eyebrows shot up. "Harlequin always kisses Columbine."

"Not at a tryout!"

"No? Well, no one informed me of such a rule. Possibly because you just now made it up."

"Even you," she said between clinched teeth, "must realize that these are not ordinary circumstances. Don't you have any sense at all of self-preservation? Kissing Miss Hartland was bound to reveal your identity."

"Hardly. Not behind that infernally hot mask."

"The mask has nothing to say in the matter."

"It has everything to say. Between it and my India-ink head of hair, my own mother wouldn't know me. If she were still alive, that is."

"Don't play the naive innocent. Of course Miss Hartland knew you. How could she not? Don't pretend that all kisses are the same."

"I am not pretending. I would, for instance, know yours anywhere. But Miss Hartland has no basis for comparison."

She stared at him, incredulous. "Are you funning?"

"Certainly not."

"But I thought you and she—"

"Had an understanding? Well, everyone seemed to assume that, including Miss Hartland. Or so I thought at the time." His voice had taken on a hard edge. "But in actuality, I had never gone down upon one knee."

"And you have never kissed her? I'll not believe it."

"Well, you can believe it. She is, in fact, quite the proper miss. Or was, at any rate," he qualified, recalling the scene in the moonlit garden. "You saw how miscast she was as Columbine."

"Whereas I, I collect, am playing to type?" Persey sounded dangerous.

"Oh, Lord," he groaned, and sat up. "I did not mean that. There was no intent to make comparisons. I was simply pointing out that Miss Hartland has been brought up quite strictly. It is not unusual, so I understand, for Casanova fathers to guard their daughters like fire-breathing dragons."

"Whereas everyone knows that *actress* and *wanton* are interchangeable terms."

"Do not put words in my mouth." His anger was mounting, partially from guilt. The vision of his uncle seemed to have sprung, frowning, in between them. "Perhaps I did take advantage of the situation tonight. After all, there have to be some extra benefits to the actor's life. The money, for the most part, is trifling."

The joke fell flat. She was still seething.

"Besides," he persevered, "kissing Miss Hartland did have the desired effect. You saw how quickly she dropped her acting aspirations."

"Due entirely to pressure from her father and Mr. Warren."

"Possibly. But the fact remains, my action did get rid of her. And had we been thrown together for the next several days on such intimate terms, she no doubt would have recognized me eventually.

"And by the bye," he added dryly, "I am more than a little touched that you are so concerned with hiding my identity."

Persey recalled belatedly that she was not supposed to know the real reason for his disguise. "Well, the truth is that I deeply resent having been used."

"Used? I don't follow."

"You obviously wished to make love to Miss Hartland. Ergo, not to make the fact too obvious, you also found it necessary to kiss me."

"Oh, for God's sake." He rose to his feet and headed for the door. "*Ergo* indeed. May the Almighty deliver me from a female's logic."

"Well, I don't hear you denying it."

"Why should I bother?" He opened the door. "Did it not occur to you that it could just as easily have been the other way around?"

Having delivered this Parthian shot, he closed the door behind him. Then cursed himself for a fool all the way to his bedchamber.

Persey, meanwhile, stood staring at the closed door for several seconds, then slowly turned and began to prepare for bed. In a kind of daze, she went through the ritual of cleaning her teeth and giving her hair one hundred strokes. But even after she had climbed into the four-poster and blown out the candle, she knew that falling asleep would be beyond her capabilities. Her head was in too big a whirl.

Mr. Drury—Harlequin—Lord Worth—whoever—had sneered at her use of logic. Even so, Persey made an effort to bring that faculty into play. She might be a mere pantomime actress with an ancestry that was partially obscure, but she knew that she did not lack intelligence. So why was she reacting to this particular member of the ton like some daft, love-starved upstairs maid?

True, he was handsome. But she had often been

pursued by handsome men. Perhaps his station in life was the attraction. Being a peer of the realm was a definite romantic asset. But a *disgraced* peer of the realm? A coward? Oh, she could easily understand why Worth's first kiss had sent her swooning like some naive stage shepherdess wooed by the hero of the piece. But that was before she knew the terrible truth about him. So how to account for the fact that the second experience, before all those tonish witnesses, including the woman he loved, had had an even more devastating effect?

Persey flipped over on her stomach, pulled the pillow over her head, and tried to crowd out the troubling thoughts with fleecy sheep. One. Two. Three. Four. She did not hear her chamber door creak open.

Lord Worth did, however. His attempts at sleep had been no more successful than Persey's. And given the fact that he had far more reason for mental turmoil than she, he had given up the struggle and risen to sit by the open window and blow a cloud. His mind was occupied, and at first he thought he had imagined the stealthy footsteps going down the hall. But then there was no mistaking the slow creaking of the door.

"Blast!" He was on his feet, grabbing his dressing gown from the bedpost and shrugging into it as he hurried out his door. "Blast!" he repeated silently as he returned to his dressing table to slap the Harlequin mask in place and tie its ribbons. He stubbed his toe against a chair leg in the darkness and cursed, but mutely as his new persona called for.

* * *

Lady Lavinia had had no difficulty in falling asleep. Philosophically, she held insomnia in contempt, tending to blame the condition upon bad conscience. "The sleep of the just" was no idle phrase in her ladyship's mind.

But by the same token, she slept like a good watchdog, alert to any activities around her. And it was not by chance that she had placed herself in the room next to the one assigned to Colonel Hartland.

For she did not think well of the colonel. Nor did she believe for a moment that all of his passion for the theater was art directed. Though there were many in Lady Lavinia's set who would turn a deaf ear toward midnight trysts, her ladyship was not like-minded. If she had any say in the matter, Colonel Hartland would not turn Habersham Hall into a bordello.

She eased quietly out of bed, donned her dressing gown, straightened her nightcap, and slowly turned her doorknob, the only one, thanks to her orders, in the stately home that did not squeak. She peered down the hall just as the colonel's candle turned the corner. She followed stealthily.

Persey was just beginning to drift into sleep when her bed tilted from the weight of another body crawling into it. At first she thought that her drowsy mind was lulling her into the kind of dream her conscious thoughts would never allow. Columbine was just ready to welcome Harlequin with open arms when consciousness—and conscience—returned. The pillow went flying off her head as she flipped upright. "What are you doing back here?" she snapped.

"Shhh," the colonel cautioned, and put one hand

gently over her mouth while he pulled her against his night-shirted chest. Persey's eyes grew wild in the candlelight as she realized her mistake. She bit the hand and, as it was jerked away, gave tongue.

Her *"help!"* though benefiting from a trained actress's gift for projection, turned out to be superfluous. Lord Worth had already bounded into the room and had a firm grip upon the colonel's nightshirt collar. He gave a jerk that propelled the military man off the bed, where he somehow managed to land, catlike, upon his feet. Worth immediately altered this position with a leveler that sent the colonel sprawling upon the large cabbage roses woven into the carpet. "Arrr!" He growled with satisfaction at a job well done before pausing to consider whether a mute could have managed even that much utterance.

The colonel's ejection from the bed had managed to sweep his candle from the night table. Lady Lavinia, who had arrived in time to view all the action, now leaped to retrieve it from the floor, where it lay upon its side, the flame sputtering in a spilled pool of wax. "You could burn down the house, you know," she chided.

"My word!" Persey gasped from her kneeling position upon the bed. "Are there any more visitors to come? Perhaps I should ring for tea."

Chapter
Fourteen

LADY LAVINIA DID NOT RETURN DIRECTLY TO HER BED. After delivering the colonel to his and listening to his explanation of his sleepwalking proclivity ("That dumb-show Harlequin was completely out of line. I've a mind to ask Newbright to send him packing"), she headed for Jane's bedchamber, tapped softly on the door, and entered.

Jane, no light sleeper, had to be shaken awake even after Lavinia had lighted her bedside candle. "Wha's wrong?" she asked foggily as she sat up.

"Nothing. I simply wish to ask you something. Could you describe Lord Worth for me?"

"Could I what?" Jane was beginning to awaken. She stared at her friend in disbelief. "Could I what? What time is it, anyway?"

"One o'clock. I realize you saw Lord Worth only from across the theater. But jog your memory. If asked what he looked like, what would be his most striking feature?"

"Lavinia, could this not wait until morning? I was asleep. You are without a doubt the most inconsiderate— Well, never mind." She cut off the diatribe with a sigh. Sad experience told her she would not divert or shame her friend. Better to bend to her wishes and hope to be allowed her rest.

"Oh, very well. As you have said, my view was from a distance, but he was obviously quite handsome."

"Can you not be more specific? What stands out in your memory?"

"His hair. Fair enough to be almost white."

"Excellent. What else?"

"Fine, wide-spaced eyes. I could not say as to their color."

"What else?"

"Oh, my heavens. I did not intend to do his portrait, you know. I simply looked and he registered in my mind as nice-looking. For all the usual reasons, I collect. Good features—a well-molded face—high forehead—cleft chin."

"Ahhh." Lady Lavinia smiled with satisfaction. "Are you quite sure, Jane, about the chin?"

"Why, yes," her friend replied thoughtfully. "I must be, or else why would I have thought about it?"

"Why indeed. You have been most helpful. There is something I must check with Addie, but I suppose in view of the hour, it can wait till morning. I will leave you now. Sleep well."

"Sleep well!" Jane muttered through clenched teeth as the door closed. What makes Addie so fortunate? She thumped her pillows against the headboard and reached for her book.

Lady Lavinia, her mystery now ninety-nine percent solved, went to sleep with her customary alacrity.

Lord Worth was too troubled to do likewise. He had tossed and turned, wrestling with problems, and was finally consigning them all to the devil and losing consciousness when a small detail out of the eventful evening tweaked his memory. He had washed off his makeup before retiring. Could the colonel have possibly noticed the difference? He doubted it. The altercation had been too fast. And after he had floored the colonel, he would have been far too dazed to notice a slight difference in the contour of a chin. No, that was the least of his worries. Lord Worth rolled to his other side and drifted off to sleep.

Persey, whose night's sleep had been fitful to say the least, had been relieved to be the only house guest in the breakfast parlor. She was just helping herself to kidneys at the sideboard, however, when Lady Lavinia entered. It was all she could do to suppress a sigh. Her good-morning was not entirely free of embarrassment. She would have liked to put last night's dust-up out of her mind.

Lady Lavinia suffered from no such inhibitions. After she had heaped her plate and joined Persey at the breakfast table, she came directly to the point. "Am I right, Miss McCall, in assuming that you have not encouraged Colonel Hartland in his amorous pursuit?"

"I most certainly have not."

"No need to climb into the boughs. I thought as much. But I do feel I should warn you that he is a notorious rake with a penchant for actresses. However, he tells me that he was merely sleepwalking last night and that the incident was entirely innocent on his part."

"Oh, indeed?"

"That is what he says. Still, I find it providential that your Harlequin was so protective. The situation could have become—awkward. By the bye"—she tried for casualness—"has Mr. Drury been with your company long? I do not recall seeing his name listed on the playbill."

"Oh, yes." Persey was not misled by the studied "by the bye." Her thumbs began to prick. "He has been at the Wells for donkey's years. He understudies our senior Harlequin and works backstage. Scenic effects are his specialty."

"Well, I must say that you are fortunate to have such a knight errant with you. He was certainly Johnny-on-the-spot. He is amazingly conscientious."

Persey had the good actress's sensitivity to nuances and was aware that she was being probed. But to what end, she could not say. Nor did she stop to analyze the protective instinct that caused her to reply, "It is not at all amazing, actually. You see, he is my husband."

Lady Lavinia choked on her bite of ham. Then took a long, slow draft of tea. "Well now, I am most amazed. I had no idea. You are, are you not, called *Miss* McCall?"

"Yes. That was Piccolo's decision. And though I objected, he was adamant. He feels that the unmarried state is better for business."

"I see."

Lady Lavinia looked at her thoughtfully.

Persey was of two minds about informing "Mr. Drury" of his new status. Since he was a mute, it was hardly likely that he would make any contradictory blunder, but still— It seemed only fair to fill him in.

He was not in his chamber, however. "Oh, blast!" She feared that he had gone wandering again, a risky business with three close acquaintances on the premises. But when she entered her own bedchamber, he found him, dressed in his borrowed day clothes, reclining on her bed, consuming tea and Bath cakes, and licking his fingers.

"Do make yourself at home," she said witheringly.

"Thank you, I am. You've certainly taken your time with breakfast. Peckish, were you?"

A thought just struck as she closed the door behind her. "Where is your mask?"

"Right here." He pulled it from his pocket and waved it at her.

"Then why did you not clap it on when you saw the door open? I might have been the maid. Or anybody."

"Not a chance. I certainly know your step by now."

"Oh."

"But speaking of 'anybody,' how is the dear colonel this morning?"

"I couldn't say. Only Lady Lavinia was in the breakfast parlor when I was there."

"I hope the randy old goat has a headache strong enough to dampen his lechery a bit. And for God's sake, don't encourage him when he recovers."

"I never did!" She glared indignantly.

"You never did *intentionally*. But just looking the way you do is enough to set him off."

"Then perhaps I should be the one to wear the mask." She reached out for it.

"Very amusing. But I am warning you seriously. You can't even be civil with a man like Hartland without his thinking you want to—get cozy. And I'll say it again: Don't think for a moment he has marriage in mind."

"Oh, I am well aware that he has no such intention. And even if he might once have had the notion, he is fast discarding it. For I collect that just about now Lady Lavinia is informing him that I am already married."

He choked.

Ham or cake, this reaction to her change in status no longer came as a surprise. She waited patiently for the slow, restorative intake of tea.

His hand shook a little as it held the cup, and, if she had noticed, he had grown a trifle pale. "You are actually married?"

"So I just informed Lady Lavinia."

He did not really need to ask the question, but he did so anyway.

"And who is the fortunate husband?"

"Why, you, as a matter of fact."

Chapter Fifteen

"A DELAIDE, DO YOU RECALL ANY SCANDAL CONCERN-
ing the late Lord Worth?"

Lady Lavinia had left the breakfast parlor to go
straight to her cousin's room. She believed in coming directly to the point.

Addie, who was seated at a small rosewood desk
penning a letter to her special friend, Colonel
Marston, looked up and frowned thoughtfully. She
did not seem to find the question at all odd.

"Scandal? Are you thinking that the present Lord
Worth inherited that tendency from his father? I
would not think so. I did not know his late lordship
personally, of course, but it was my impression that
he kept himself to himself, that he disliked town
ways and preferred to spend his time on his estate.
Still, I collect," she mused, "that one can have scan-
dals in the country."

Lady Lavinia sat down in a wing chair and carefully selected a chocolate from an open box on the table beside it. "Perhaps *scandal* is too strong a word. *Odd* could be more apt. Was there not something the least bit odd about his marriage?"

Addie brightened. "Why, I do believe you are right. Fancy remembering it for all these years. The *on-dit* was that he had married some actress. Which was completely out of character for such a proper type. That family is quite high in the instep, you know. As I recall, they put the word out that the bride was reared abroad. But people still whispered that she was an actress."

"Ah!" Lady Lavinia breathed in satisfaction. "Thank you, Addie. You have been of great assistance." She helped herself to another chocolate and left her cousin to her correspondence.

Lord Worth was of two minds about Persey's deception, and said so. "Passing as your husband should help hide my identity, but I'm not sure that Piccolo will be any too pleased."

They were on their way to the theater with his lordship once more in full Harlequin costume.

"Why wouldn't he be? You don't deny that he asked you to look after me?"

"No, I don't deny it. But I hardly think that pretending to be man and wife was what he had in mind."

She gave him a level look. "We are not going to pretend too hard, you understand."

His mask hid any reaction. "I realize that. But you haven't thought about Piccolo's feelings. There is quite an age difference, you know. It makes a man rather—touchy—they say."

"Oh, Piccolo knows that the colonel's not the first over-the-hill male to come sniffing around me. I doubt he'll be the last. So why should he object to my throwing a bit of cold water on him?"

Worth couldn't decide whether she was deliberately misinterpreting what he had said or not. Perhaps in her mind there was no age difference between her and Piccolo. Love affected people in odd ways. Or so he'd heard.

The colonel was already onstage waiting for them and looking ill at ease. He made a gruff apology for the unfortunate sleepwalking incident of the night before which Persey accepted graciously while Harlequin stood mutely by. "And my husband regrets attacking you. He quite misunderstood, you see." She lowered her voice. "The fact is," she stage-whispered, "his disfigurement has made him quite prone to jealousy."

Two dark eyes impaled her through the mask.

They worked intensely for the next two hours while Persey led the other two through their comic paces. She congratulated herself for having rendered her fellow actor mute. Since she was, by necessity, required to give all the stage directions, the colonel was not to know that the professional Harlequin was actually as great a novice as himself.

"In the Pantomime, timing is everything," she kept repeating as Pantaloon responded too quickly to some provocation from the other two. "Pause before you react. Let the audience catch up. First build suspense. Then comes the action."

She was impressed that Lord Worth was such a quick study. No one in the house party, she felt sure, would suspect that he was a novice. Then she recalled the intense way he had studied the action from the stage box. It was certainly paying off, she concluded.

The colonel was not nearly so adept. And as a

Piccolo surrogate, the burden of the performance fell upon him. He, too, had memorized the Pantomime, up to a point. He did know what was expected. It was how to do it that eluded him. Actors' instinct was undoubtedly a gift, Persey thought as she patiently walked the colonel through a piece of business counting out the beats as though she were teaching him the waltz. But she gave him due credit. He was determined to learn. There was more to his devotion to the Pantomime than a penchant for pretty women.

Then things began to click into place. Pantaloon chased Harlequin and Columbine through a series of comic misadventures, deceiving and being deceived, robbing and being robbed, thrashing and being thrashed till at last they stood together downstage, panting with exhaustion.

There was the sound of clapping. Lady Lavinia, who, unobserved, had taken a backseat in the auditorium and watched the action grow from its stumbling start to its present polish, now came forward. Her presence startled the actors in more ways than one. Lord Worth was aided by his mask, but Miss McCall and Colonel Hartland both had to struggle to keep their astonishment from being reflected in their faces when they saw her regalia.

She was wearing the costume she had designed for the Pickering Club, which consisted of voluminous Turkish trousers topped with a smocklike overblouse. She had said that the ensemble was inspired by the pageboy outfit favored by Lady Caroline Lamb several years before, when she had been in hot pursuit of Lord Byron. Jane had remarked that it made them look like retirees from some *Arabian Nights* seraglio.

Whatever the costume's origins, Lady Lavinia

now strode forward with a complete lack of self-consciousness. "Bravo," she said with sincerity and, perhaps, the desire to pour oil upon troubled waters. "Colonel, you were excellent. Not up to Piccolo's standards, naturally"—Total honesty was one of her ladyship's worst qualities—"but most amusing nonetheless."

In spite of the qualifier, the colonel was pleased. "Why, thank you, ma'am," he said gruffly.

"I heartily agree with Lady Lavinia." Persey turned to the colonel while Lord Worth longed to kick her. With one charming smile she was rekindling the colonel's cooled-off ardor. "You have accomplished wonders. Now, I collect, we all deserve a rest."

"That is certainly true," her ladyship said apologetically, "but I was hoping Mr. Drury would rehearse the sword fight with me. That is, if he is not too fatigued. It is too much to ask, sir?"

The masked man mutely bowed his willingness.

"And if you, Miss McCall—by the bye, is it proper to call you 'Miss McCall' or do you prefer being addressed offstage as Mrs. Drury?"

"Miss McCall is quite acceptable."

This reminder of the pretty actress's marital status seemed to bring the colonel back down to earth. "If you will excuse me," he murmured, "my daughter is waiting for me."

"As I was about to say," her ladyship continued after the colonel had left, "I do not like to detain you further, Miss McCall, but since your husband here is—er—voiceless, if you could just outline a course of action for us before you go, we should be able to carry on quite well."

"Why, yes, of course. First tell me, though, have

you had any experience with this sort of thing, your ladyship?"

Her closest friends, realizing that Lavinia never lacked for confidence in any situation, would not have been impressed by her "Oh, yes, indeed."

Persey was. She skipped over the rudiments of swordplay and went straight to the routine that she herself had used to initiate "Mr. Drury" at Sadler's Wells. (When she came to the window dive, he shifted uneasily and made a firm resolution to tip his catchers substantially before the performance.) "Are there any questions?" she asked when she'd concluded. Upon being assured that all was perfectly clear, she excused herself. "I promised to write Piccolo the details of our production," she explained.

As Persey left the auditorium, Lord Worth walked off into the wings and returned with two swords. He handed one to her ladyship with a bow, then took his place upon the mark Persey had indicated as their starting point. Lady Lavinia followed and assumed a martial stance.

Harlequin raised his sword. "En garde," he mouthed. Lady Lavinia brandished her weapon in reply.

Noise being an important feature of a stage fight, he hit the flat side of her sword with a mighty clash. The blow sent that weapon sailing out of her hand, across the floats, and onto the front row.

Oh, God, he mutely groaned as he jumped down after it, trying not to think of the damage that could have been done to any member of the audience unfortunate enough to be sitting there. He retrieved the weapon and climbed back onstage, where he tried to mime an apology for the force of his blow.

"The fault was entirely my own," her ladyship said graciously as he returned the sword to her. Then, knowing the value of surprise, Lavinia lunged immediately for his chest. His providential parry sent the sword sailing across the footlights once again.

It was a fortunate thing that Lord Worth had taken the vow of silence. The stream of expletives rushing through his mind as he once again jumped down from the stage were not the sort of thing one voiced in the presence of a lady. This time, thanks to the desperation of the reflex action that had saved him from being skewered, the sword had made it to the second row of chairs.

"Hmmm," Lady Lavinia mused as he climbed once more back upon the stage and handed her the weapon. "This is not as simple as it looks. And, yes, you are right in what you are thinking, Mr. Drury. I have never done this sort of thing before. The 'experience' that I claimed came only from observation. Execution seems to be an entirely different matter."

Lord Worth, being a stranger to Lady Lavinia, mistook this speech for capitulation. He reached for her sword, preparing to return it to the property box.

"Give up?" Her tone was indignant. "Indeed not! You shall simply have to treat me like the novice that I am and take me through the routine slowly, step by step."

Oh, God, Worth groaned—or prayed—inwardly once more. This was worse than the blind leading the blind. At least the blind were only out for a stroll and not fooling around with lethal weapons. How was a stage-novice mute supposed to teach the art of stage swordplay to an antique lady?

He mimed the danger in what they were doing by applying his finger to the sword point and jerking it away, then sucking imaginary blood.

"I do realize the hazards, young man," she said dryly, "but if you are thinking of wooden swords"—He was—"dismiss the thought. I saw Mrs. Wybrow onstage several years ago demonstrating her prowess with the sword, and what another female can do so skillfully is certainly within my grasp. And no, it is not necessary to recall Miss McCall—Mrs. Drury, that is—to interpret for us." Lady Lavinia had developed, Lord Worth realized, an uncanny ability to read his mind. "If you will simply guide me through this slowly, step by step and blow by blow, I am confident that I shall soon be able to master it."

He capitulated. First he showed her how to grasp her weapon properly, then demonstrated, with a view toward self-preservation, the importance that illusion played. When apparently skewering one's opponent, the technique was to pass him by (the illusion aided by a quick turn of the other's body), and give the appearance of having done so while the fellow-actor remained unpunctured. Next, he led her, carefully, through the art of thrust and parry, with much clash of weapons and stamping of feet on his part and throaty cries on hers to give the appearance of fierce battle.

He was impressed—both with her determination and her stamina. And at the end of two hours he was convinced that they would be able to create a quite credible battle scene, if not quite up to the fabled Mrs. Wybrow's standards, certainly effective enough to entertain a bucolic audience. He smiled his congratulations as he waved them to a halt.

Lady Lavinia, trying not to betray her fatigue by

gasping for breath, pulled a handkerchief out of the recesses of her billowing trousers in order to mop her gleaming brow. As she did so, she somehow managed to dislodge an enameled snuffbox—a rather surprising thing for her to be carrying since she abhorred tobacco—and send it rolling across the stage. Lord Worth courteously tracked it down, then bent over to retrieve it. As he did so, the sharp point of Lady Lavinia's weapon pricked him on the rear.

"Damnation!"

He leaped upright and whirled around.

"Why, Mr. Drury," Lady Lavinia beamed. "You have uttered. It is a miracle!"

Chapter
Sixteen

LORD WORTH'S MIND WAS IN A TURMOIL. HE HAD
thought that a walk around the artificial lake
might restore his brain to some kind of rationality.
But in spite of a glorious day when the sun made
the water sparkle and the butterflies chase one another (while nervously looking over their shoulders
for Lord Newbright and his net), it hadn't happened. He was at a loss as to what he should do.
When he had first arrived at the Hall, he had
hoped to manage a private word with his cousin.
But after witnessing the passionate embrace in the
garden, he was seriously questioning Clarence's di-
vided loyalty. And now that Lady Lavinia had discovered that his dumbness was a hoax, how long
would it take that shrewd lady to penetrate his disguise? Habersham Hall was clearly not the sanctu-
ary his uncle had imagined.

He was far too preoccupied to hear the sound of

soft pursuit. Or to know that he was under observation from an upstairs window by a pair of narrowed eyes. He slowed down his pace a bit, hoping his mind would take a clue from his legs and switch to calm deliberation. That did not happen. But it did give an opportunity for Miss Pamela Hartland to overtake him.

"Oh, Harlequin!"

Startled, he spun around and, before he caught himself, had almost answered. Instead, he gave her a tentative smile.

She took it for encouragement. "May I join you?" She hurried to his side. "It is a lovely day for a walk, is it not?" He nodded, and they proceeded around the lake.

It was obvious that she was very ill at ease. This noted fact did little to calm his own apprehension, though reason told him that any young lady would be nervous strolling with a masked mute of a different social order.

At first it appeared that she had been struck as dumb as he, but then she seemed to gather her resolve. "The thing is, Harlequin, I have been longing to talk with you." She colored as she realized her gaffe. "Not talk *with* you exactly—since you cannot— But we should be able to communicate— in spite of—should we not?" The lovely eyes looked up at him earnestly. He swallowed and nodded.

They were approaching the gazebo. "Oh, could we not sit a moment? I collect I should find it easier to say what I have to say." Without waiting for his consent, she headed for the shelter.

His instincts told him to beat a hasty retreat, but his curiosity overrode self-preservation. He followed her into the wooden octagon, where lattice work and intertwining vines not only offered shade but privacy. She sat down upon the bench that ran the circumference of the walls, after first dusting it with a handkerchief in deference to her pale lilac gown. He followed suit, careful to put considerable distance between them. She closed the gap.

"I feel that I must tell you"—she gazed earnestly at the masked face—"that I know your secret."

He gulped, but the habit of speechlessness prevailed. Or perhaps he had truthfully been rendered mute from shock. His eyes, however, must have betrayed his state of mind, for she reached out a trembling hand and placed it upon his. "But have no fear. I will never betray you. I wish only to help."

He weakly smiled his gratitude and was groping for words to convey it, when she preempted his chance to respond. "For some things cannot be hidden, can they? The mask can do only so much. Your secret was out, you see, the moment you kissed me."

Dear Lord, Persey was right. But how could it have happened since he had never—

"I knew immediately then that you had developed a deep passion for me. That you had doubtlessly loved me from the moment you first saw me. It was inevitable, I collect, given the circumstances. I know you did not intend to betray yourself, but it was all there in your kiss. The thwarted drive of a virile man—perhaps once handsome?—now too hideous to show his face to the world—for a beauti— that is to say, a *passable* young woman who is far above his touch. Oh, my dear sir, it almost broke my heart. I have thought of little since. And I have at last realized how I can help you. If you will allow me to look upon your face, and if you then perceive that I can look below the surface and see through the disfigurement to the soul, then, even though your love for me can never bear fruition because of our different stations, it could make you see that some other woman of your own class could love you for yourself."

Good Lord, he thought, she is doing *Beauty and the Beast*. He made a choking sound that came perilously close to a growl.

"Besides"—there was admiration in her voice—"your physique is quite exceptional, you know." She leaned closer, her hands clasped beseechingly, her pose romantic, drawn no doubt from some Gothic illustration.

For his part, Lord Worth was busily practicing what she had preached. He was seeing through all that lovely surface. She really is the complete ninnyhammer, he thought, and was on the point of congratulating himself for a narrow escape, when she flung her arms around him. Before he was able to extricate himself in a gentlemanly fashion, her lips were devouring his own in a manner that brought such expressions as *light skirt* and *jade* to mind.

At first he was too astonished by the sensual side to the proper Miss Hartland to do more than cooperate. He snapped back to reality only when he realized that she was fumbling with the strings that held his mask in place. He shifted her unceremoniously from his lap and leaped to his feet.

"Oh, you must not be afraid," she pleaded. "Allow me to gaze upon your face. I shall not be shocked. I promise you."

Would you care to wager? he thought as he backed toward the door. But in actual reply he sadly shook his head, a tragic figure, sparing her, and him, the worst. He was both proud of and appalled by his performance. Could the actor so easily swallow up the man? he was wondering when a shadow fell across the door and his cousin Clarence stepped inside.

"Ah, here you are, Pamela. I have been looking everywhere for you." Mr. Warren's face was darkened with suspicion. The look he bent upon the actor was not friendly.

Thankful that he was not required to come up with some spoken lame excuse for being alone in a gazebo with the beauty (who could not have looked more guilty even if Mr. Warren had entered a moment earlier), Worth bowed stiffly and hurried back toward the safety of the house.

He was relieved to find the theater empty. And surprised. For though he had developed a hearty dislike for Colonel Hartland, in one area he granted the man a grudging respect. He did indeed love the Pantomime, a love that might include the dressing rooms of its female performers but went well beyond that penchant. He could be usually found onstage, seriously and happily working on some element of his performance. But for the moment, at least, Worth had the place all to himself.

He needed to think. He realized as much. He needed to try to make sense of the scene he had just been through as well as to decide what future course to take. But he also realized that from the moment he began to rehearse his act, mastering it would absorb him utterly.

Since attending the Pantomime as a child, he had always known that he was fascinated by the acrobatics of the clowns. And, as he had demonstrated to Piccolo, after each visit to Sadler's Wells he had worked diligently to master some trick that had especially impressed him. But at the time this preoccupation had seemed no different from the hours spent in perfecting swimming or cricket. Now he knew better. Nothing matched the intoxication of performing before an audience. Even as the ignominious vegetable man he had found that out. And now, in spite of all his difficulties, he was keenly looking forward to the performance here. Was it something in his blood after all?

Worth carefully tested the rope strung high above the auditorium before he mounted it. Tightrope walking was something he had mastered as a child, but time and growth had made him rusty. Now, though, he had reached a level of proficiency that left him dissatisfied with merely traversing the auditorium over the spectators' heads. He had crossed the room and was on his way back toward the stage, plotting a handstand, when suddenly the tightrope jerked. While he strove to maintain his balance, the rope went slack beneath him. As he fell, he grabbed it with both hands and rode it like a swinging grapevine to drop catlike upon the stage and whirl to face the auditorium.

His cousin Clarence was climbing down from the ladder that gave access to a high hook on the back wall, where one end of the rope had been fastened. The congratulatory smile upon his face was not pleasant. Worth realized that he was looking at a stranger. Changing one's social class brought with it a whole new perspective. Educational, no doubt, but unsettling. "Well done, scarface," Mr. Warren mocked as he walked slowly down the center aisle toward the stage.

The performer bowed.

"Next time, however, you might not be so fortunate. Consider this a polite warning."

An exaggerated gesture communicated complete bewilderment.

"Oh, you understand me very well, scarface. Stay away from Miss Hartland if you value your life."

The two men were too intent upon each other to notice Persey's quiet entrance. She paused at the auditorium doorway, taking in the dangling rope, the blatant hostility.

Harlequin gave an exaggerated mocking recoil, then walked back to pick up one of the two swords propped against the upstage wall and flourished it invitingly.

"I'll not fence with you," the other growled.

Then, lacking the actual object, Harlequin mimed loading a pistol which he pointed toward the other's chest.

Warren looked contemptuous. "You fail to get my meaning, scarface. A gentleman does not duel with common scum. So listen carefully. If you so much as look at Miss Hartland again through that clown's mask of yours, I'll have you beaten into an inch of your life. What price a crippled acrobat, scarface?"

He wheeled and walked rapidly back up the aisle, brushing past Miss McCall with only a cool nod to acknowledge her shocked presence.

She hurried toward the stage, where Worth was propping Lady Lavinia's sword in place. "What was that all about?" she demanded as he turned to face her.

He shrugged.

"Dammit, answer me! I happen to know you can talk, remember?"

He grinned beneath his mask. "Does Piccolo know that you swear like a sailor? He's quite a stickler for propriety, I've been told. Among the ladies, at any rate. That sort of language could cost you a sizable fine. Not that I'll tell, of course."

"Don't change the subject. I heard that man threaten you. What is this all about?" She gestured toward the dangling rope. "Were you on that thing when it came loose?"

"As a matter of fact, yes."

She turned pale. "Oh, dear heavens. You might have been killed."

"Maimed, more likely. I think that was the general idea. Well, you heard."

"You mean Mr. Warren unhooked the rope? With you on it? On purpose?"

He gave a nod to each question. Persey felt a sudden need to sit down. "Fine friends you have," she said weakly as she collapsed into a front row chair.

"I take it that the gorgeous Miss Hartland is the bone of contention," she observed after a charged silence.

He shrugged.

"I told you to stop that," she snapped.

"Sorry. Well, yes, you are right. He does seem to take a rather—proprietary—position where she is concerned."

"I thought you were going to keep away from her." She struggled to keep her voice neutral. "That proved too big a strain, I take it. I knew no good would come from that kiss."

"Which one?"

"Don't try to be funny. I don't understand you at all. Well, I do in a way. She *is* lovely. *Dazzling* is probably the word for her. And that seems to be all that men really care about. So the fact that she wants no more to do with you now that you are"—

she collected herself just before uttering the word 'disgraced' and substituted—"*penniless* doesn't actually weigh with you, does it?"

"Ah, but you—and our Mr. Warren—quite mistake the matter. I don't wish to appear immodest, but it is Miss Hartland who has been pursuing me, not vice versa. She has a mission, you see," he grinned. "She wishes to rehabilitate Harlequin."

Chapter Seventeen

*E*ACH DAY LORD WORTH WAITED EAGERLY FOR THE ARrival of the post. He was usually the first to shuffle through the stack of correspondence placed in the hall upon a silver tray. After every disappointment he found himself questioning the judgment of leaving his fate in the hands of an uncle he scarcely knew.

But now, finally, here was a folded missive with the words *Mr. Drury, Habersham Hall* scrawled upon it. He snatched the letter up and hurried back to his bedchamber to break the seal in private and read the contents.

The process did not take long. Piccolo used only a few lines to say that the former Bow Street Runner whom he'd hired to look into "the matter we discussed" had so far had little success. He would not relax his diligence, however. In the meantime Mr. Drury would be gratified to hear that the victim was improving daily. "With warmest regards to Persephone," he remained, etc.

Worth crumpled the letter into a ball and tossed it toward his reflection in the looking glass. He then took advantage of his solitude to curse aloud, long and eloquently, albeit softly.

Had he not been so intent upon his own affairs, Worth might have noticed another letter among the stack of correspondence on the tray addressed in the same hand as the one he had received. For in answer to certain inquiries upon her part, Piccolo had also written Lady Lavinia. What he had to say cast her into a brown study that lasted throughout the day.

Indeed she remained far too occupied during the evening meal to pay attention to the moods of the other diners. Under different circumstances she might have found certain departures from their normal behavior interesting. Lord Newbright, for instance, was not his usual taciturn self but was talking to Mrs. Abingdon in a quite animated fashion. His conversation was punctuated with gestures, mostly indicating flight, that were placing his long-stemmed wineglass in grave peril. Since little was required of her save an occasional intelligent question whenever his lordship's discourse began to flag, Jane was able to make a hearty meal of potted shrimp, sole with wine, roast beef, and apple puffs. (No departure from normal behavior here.)

Colonel Hartland, who for the most part had left off his pursuit of Miss McCall after learning of the "marriage," was preoccupied. He was plotting a transformation that would electrify the audience to take place during the Pantomime.

Addie had seized the opportunity provided by the

colonel's silence to eagerly question Miss McCall about the private lives of various luminaries of the stage. Although Persey replied politely to the best of her ability, it became obvious even to Addie that her mind was elsewhere. She, too, lapsed into silence after a while.

But had there been a prize awarded to the most unconvivial diner, it would have gone without a doubt to Mr. Warren. That young gentleman had spent the evening rearranging his food and replying only in monosyllables to Miss Hartland's scattered attempts at conversation. If anyone besides the beauty had bothered to notice, which they did not, he was in a high ill humor.

Whether it was Miss Hartland's intent to fan the flames of his jealousy by the mention of a certain name, or whether she was merely trying to do the proper by rescuing the meal from social disaster, even she probably could not have said. But for whatever reason, she gazed down the table and asked politely, "Tell us, Lady Lavinia, how are you and Mr. Drury progressing with your swordfighting exhibition?"

Lavinia was snatched back into the present. She ceased crumbling the roll she had been working on and answered politely. "It is shaping up quite nicely, thank you."

"Curst business, if you ask me," her brother stopped his monologue on the American Monarch butterfly to say. "Women have no business with swords. Bound to get hurt. Man's business."

The colonel snapped out of his reverie to join the conversation. "Well, sir, while I agree with you on principle, there is precedent for what her ladyship is doing. Other females have engaged in swordplay upon the stage and received considerable acclaim for their efforts. Mrs. Wybrow, of course, springs to mind. I cannot help but believe, though," he chuckled, "that the appeal lies more in the novelty than the proficiency. It's another case of Dr. Johnson's dog walking on its hind legs. It's not that these ladies fence well. The remarkable thing is that they do it at all."

Most of the diners chuckled at the tired old chestnut, but Jane gazed at her friend with apprehension, braced for an explosion. But while she did observe the warning signs of rising choler—a reddening neck, sparks flashing from the eyes—she was amazed to see Lavinia bite off whatever setdown she was forming and substitute a smile.

"There is, I collect, at least a kernel of truth in what you say, sir." She nodded graciously. "Whereas I do insist that we swordswomen are their match in reflex and dexterity, I yield to the men in the matter of muscle. There is little doubt that, on the average, you men are our superiors in any type of combat that involves brute strength." She paused to smile once more, while Jane regarded her with growing suspicion and Addie's fork paused, en route to mouth, while she watched her friend uneasily. "That is why the invention of firearms was such a boon to women. You must admit, sir, that the pistol is a great equalizer of the sexes."

"I admit no such thing," the colonel retorted. "Oh, granted that a bullet fired by a female has the potential of doing just as much damage as a bullet fired by a male, but the unvarnished truth is, your ladyship, that the female most often misses."

The laughter of the gentlemen covered the silence of the ladies.

"Now, that, sir, is where I must differ. Firing a pistol accurately merely requires a steady hand

and a keen eye. Qualities that our sex possesses. You surely will not deny that?"

"Under some circumstances I would grant your ladyship's premise. But marksmanship also requires cool nerves and the ability not to flinch at a loud report. These qualities guarantee the steady hand that you mentioned. And, no, I do not believe that females possess such stoicism."

"Indeed?" Lady Lavinia's eyebrows rose as she leaned forward. "Shall we put our theories to the test?"

The colonel was looking amused. "And just how do you propose we do that?"

"Why, by a marksmanship contest. The ladies against the gentlemen."

"Lavinia, will you cease making a cake of yourself and eat your dinner," her brother said, frowning.

"No, no," the colonel protested. "Let her proceed. It all sounds quite diverting. What have you in mind, Lady Lavinia?"

"Well," the other mused, "in order to make this a true gender test, we need several contestants. You gentlemen will all agree to shoot?"

The colonel and Mr. Warren nodded. Her brother merely glared his disgust.

"Come, come, Newbright," she chided. "I happen to know you are an expert marksman. It is only fair to the gentleman's cause that you participate."

"Oh, very well," he replied grudgingly, and she shifted her attention. "Now then, ladies. I shall, of course, try my skill. Who else is with me?"

She looked around the table, but none of the fairer sex met her eyes. "Jane?"

"Don't be ridiculous."

"Then how about you, Adelaide? Well, no, never mind. Miss Hartland? Surely you will join me. A soldier's daughter should be a natural."

"Oh, no." The beauty looked appalled at the very notion. "I could not. Pray excuse me."

"You then, Miss McCall?"

"Since I have never fired a pistol, I fear I would do your cause more harm than good. But if you wish it, I will try."

"No, no, my dear, though I do applaud your spirit. If there are no objections, I shall be happy to take the field as the sole representative of our sex, Colonel Hartland."

"Very well, your ladyship. And to be sporting about the thing, shall we say then that if you out-shoot any one of us, the victory is yours?"

"Done. Two days hence? Weather permitting, of course."

"Done." The colonel chuckled and dug into his pudding.

The gentlemen showed no inclination to linger over their brandy and cigars but soon joined the ladies in the withdrawing room. Miss McCall had already excused herself, pleading the need to work out some staging problems. Miss Hartland was playing softly upon the pianoforte, humming to herself. Mr. Warren joined her immediately and offered to turn the pages, an offer that she graciously accepted. The colonel stood for a moment, surveying the room, then asked leave to have an early night. The three members of the Pickering Club had drawn their chairs and heads together in conversation. Lord Newbright joined them and suggested cards. He quickly commandeered Jane for his partner, leaving his sister to cope with Adelaide.

The evening of whist was a success. Lavinia played well enough to largely compensate for Addie's inability to keep track of the cards, and the match became a contest. But no amount of effort on her part sufficed to avert defeat. "Well done, Jane," his lordship beamed at the game's conclusion.

Since Miss Hartland and Mr. Warren had long since departed for a moonlight stroll, the foursome shared the tea board exclusively, a state of affairs that his lordship particularly approved of. Not only was he unable to relax among relative strangers, the company of his sister and the ladies he had known since their infantry made it possible to indulge in some plain speaking. He did so.

"Vinny, what sort of maggots do you have on the brain now?"

"I have no idea of what you mean, George. And pray do not call me Vinny."

"You know dashed well what I mean. The shooting contest. What was that all about?"

"Was it not obvious? The colonel's superiority was becoming insufferable. I felt the necessity of bringing him down a notch or so."

"Well, you picked a damned fool way to do it. The cove's bound to be a dead-eye."

"He was in the fusiliers, you know, Lavinia," Addie offered.

"I know. But I cannot see that it has much bearing upon the case."

"Oh, can you not?" her brother glared. "Then let me ask you just one question. Have you ever in your life fired a pistol?"

"Actually, no."

His lordship, Mrs. Abingdon, and Mrs. Oliver groaned in unison.

Lady Lavinia helped herself to another slice of seed cake. "I quite look forward to the experience, though," she said.

Chapter Eighteen

PERSEY WAS STANDING CENTER STAGE, HER BACK TO the auditorium and her brow furrowed in thought. She had been trying to come up with a way to achieve a bit of comic trickery without the machinery available at Sadler's Wells. She did not hear the colonel slip up behind her.

"Ah, my dear."

As his hands fell lightly upon her shoulders, she let out a yelp and whirled to face him. "Oh, Colonel Hartland, you startled me." She tried to back away, but he was now holding her more firmly.

"But you have no need to be afraid of me, my dear," he said softly. "I hold you in the highest regard. You surely must know that." She smiled weakly and attempted once more to pull away, but his grip grew tighter. "Don't try to escape me," he breathed softly in her face. She did wish he had not partaken quite so freely of the onions served at dinner. "You do owe me an explanation, you know. What you did was cruel."

"Oh? And what was that, sir?" While she had no desire to converse with this overly amorous gentleman, it seemed a better choice than what he appeared to have in mind.

"Why, not telling me that you were married. It was cruel to keep my hope alive that way."

Hope for what? she wondered. He might wish her to think he had had wedlock in mind, but she had not been born on the previous day. "I supposed you knew," she prevaricated. "I kept my maiden name only because I started my career with it. That is not unheard of in the theater, you know."

"In my experience, the opposite usually holds true." The colonel set the record straight. "Stage performers often pretend to a marriage that never took place. But what's done's done. Only tell me this, my dear. How could you have come to marry such a fellow?" There was genuine concern in his voice. "You, with your vibrant youth and beauty." He was moving his hands down from her shoulders to clasp around her back and pull her against his chest. "To be shackled for life to a scarred mute. Oh, my dear Miss McCall, how could you have done such a thing?"

She struggled to extract herself without getting him overly exercised in the process. "He was not always thus." Her words were smothered by the superfine of his shoulder. "Actually, he was once quite handsome."

"But now! How horrible for you, my lovely Miss McCall. You do deserve some happiness."

Lord Worth was not certain whether throat-clearing fell within the province of a mute. He cleared his anyway.

134

The colonel leaped away from Persey. "Ah, er, Harlequin. Well met. Miss McCall and I were just rehearsing. I was about to send for you so we could make it complete."

The mouth below the mask smiled politely as Worth strolled up the aisle to join them on the stage. But the colonel was not comfortable with the expression in the outlined eyes.

Persey, ever practical, supported Colonel Hartland in his explanation. "My chief concern is with the final scene," she said. "It seems too tame for Pantaloon merely to chase the lovers, then fall over his own feet, as it were. Though I must say, you do a most excellent fall, sir," she added to the colonel's gratification. "But I was wondering, do you suppose his lordship would allow us to cut a stage trap?"

"An excellent idea. It would make all the difference. Harlequin could wave his magic sword and I would disappear in a puff of smoke." The colonel's eyes gleamed with excitement. "I will personally ask Lord Newbright for his permission."

"Well—" Frowning, Persey considered the matter further. "I am not sure that would be the best course to take. Why don't I broach the subject to Lady Lavinia? She is bound to think it's a capital idea. And she can bully her brother into anything."

The colonel reluctantly agreed, and the matter was settled.

"Well then, shall we rehearse our final scene as if the trap were there?"

After a few run-throughs, some trial and error, and the use of imagination where the trapdoor was involved, the threesome was satisfied that the climax of their Harlequinade would be spectacular. Two of them said as much while the other remained necessarily enigmatic. It was only when they set their stage roles aside that they appeared to recall the awkward scene which "Mr. Drury" had interrupted.

"Well, I shall bid you both good night." The colonel spoke a shade too heartily. He moved as though to kiss Persey's hand, but under the stony stare emanating through the mask decided not to. Then, on his way out of the auditorium door, a muffled gasp caused him to turn back toward the stage.

They are still rehearsing was his first reaction to Harlequin and Columbine's embrace. But he quickly changed his mind. There was something too realistic by half in the way the actress's body melted into the actor's and in the way her arms clung around his neck as if she lacked the strength to support herself. And as for the masked fellow— well, if he were miming the passion of his hungry lips, then he, Colonel Spenser Hartland, was a Dutchman. He stood staring a moment longer before embarrassment overtook him. Though why he should feel like a voyeur was past all understanding. They were onstage, for the Lord's sake, were they not? He closed the auditorium door behind him with a bit more force than the operation called for.

The noise seemed to bring the couple to their senses. They moved apart to stand staring at each other, breathing heavily.

"What was that all about?" Persey finally managed to ask, using all her professional technique in the attempt to sound affronted.

If the thought did cross Worth's mind that her indignation seemed a bit overdone in view of her cooperation, the mask hid it effectively. "It was about the colonel." He gestured toward the exit.

"Well, at least you did not claim to be rehearsing. No one kisses like that onstage."

"I felt I had to make it convincing. The colonel appears to think you are starved for love. I wished to rid him of that impression."

"I see." Her voice was icy.

"Well, what else could I have done? I could hardly give him a tongue-lashing. And I hesitated to hit him. He's old enough to be my father."

And no doubt will be was her thought. But she said aloud, "Oh, I am sure you followed the only available course to make your point. How noble of you to be so self-sacrificing."

"No need to turn waspish." He was growing hot behind the mask. "I'll not deny that I enjoyed every second of it. And unless I mistake the matter, so did you." He instantly regretted the words. And not just because she had kicked him in the shins.

"That was an odious thing to say."

"Don't you ever slap?" He rubbed his leg. "That is the normal ladylike reaction."

"Well, I am neither normal nor a lady, remember? I am an actress. Besides, you would not feel it through your mask."

"Dammit, we're quarreling. Again. That is the last thing I wished to happen. Look. Will it help if I say I'm sorry?"

"Are you?"

He thought a moment, then the mouth beneath the mask broke into an impish grin. "No, not really. But I am sorry we're quarreling. Forgive me?"

He might have been an engaging little boy caught stealing sweets, she thought. Her pride refused to be seduced by his infectious smile, however. "I think it best if we simply forget the episode ever happened."

"Perhaps you're right." His mood changed to bleak seriousness. "But can one really manage that?"

"Like a shot. Just watch me."

And Persephone swept off the stage in an exit that even the great Mrs. Siddons could not have matched.

Chapter Nineteen

Mʀ. Wᴀʀʀᴇɴ ᴡᴀs ɴᴏᴛ ᴇɴᴛɪʀᴇʟʏ sᴀᴛɪsғɪᴇᴅ ᴛʜᴀᴛ ʜɪs fences were mended. Though he had apologized most humbly for his display of temper in the gazebo—"blame it upon the fact that I am mad about you and could not bear the thought of that cit approaching you in such a forward manner"—and had been graciously forgiven, he was aware that when he and Miss Hartland had strolled together through the gardens, her thoughts had been elsewhere. This accounted for the fact that after he had retired for the night, he was alert to the squeaking of her chamber door, directly across the hall from his.

He sprang out of bed and opened his own door a careful crack, then cursed himself for a suspicious fool as he saw an upstairs maid going down the hallway. He was about to close his door, when he happened to notice that she was holding a piece of paper in her hand. He eased out of his chamber to follow.

His bare feet made no sound on the hall carpet. He had no idea what he would say if someone happened to see him strolling the corridor at this hour in his nightshirt and nightcap. His luck held. And his suspicions grew as the chambermaid, instead of going toward the servants' quarters, turned the corner and headed for the wing where the actors were staying.

"You there, wait!" he snapped.

The maid let out a squeak and almost dropped her candle. "You didn't half startle me," she gasped as he closed the distance between them.

She was only about sixteen and quite pretty if one overlooked a mouthful of crooked teeth. She was also of a romantic disposition and thrilled to be carrying a note from the beautiful guest to the masked actor. Lord Newbright's residence had never been the scene of such excitement. Now here was the young lady's gentleman suitor overtaking her. She shivered, whether from fear or pleasurable excitement was debatable.

"Here, I'll take that," Mr. Warren said pleasantly as he held out his hand.

The maid thrust the note behind her back. "Oh, but I couldn't, sir. It's private like."

"Not even for a shilling—and a kiss?" (Mr. Warren was quite willing to overlook the teeth.)

The little maid looked up coquettishly. "And where would you have put a shilling in your nightshirt, sir?"

"Oh, that is no problem. I will pay you the money tomorrow. The kiss you can have tonight. Miss Hartland need never know."

She blushed and, giggling, handed him the note.

The kiss was lengthy. At its conclusion he gave the girl a dismissive pat on the bottom and she hurried away, still giggling, to tell her adventure to the tweeny who shared her attic room.

Back in his chamber Mr. Warren read the message by the candle's light. "I must see you. Meet me in the gazebo while the others are at the shooting contest. Pamela Hartland."

Mr. Warren, looking grim, thrust the paper into the candle flame and held it till it almost burned his fingers.

Lady Lavinia had made an early appointment with "Mr. Drury" for sword practice the next day. At the end of a heated forty-five minutes he mimed his satisfaction with her progress. Worth was not sure why he still kept up the pretense of being dumb. Perhaps he hoped that at her age her ladyship might have forgotten he had made that slip. Certainly she had never once referred to the incident.

Now she looked pleased at his approval. "I have had an excellent teacher. Which brings me to something I wish to ask. Can you fire a pistol?"

He nodded.

"Perhaps I should put that another way. What I am asking is, are you as proficient with the pistol as you are the sword?"

Again the masked head nodded.

"Oh, famous. Now then, could I prevail upon you to teach me the art? I need to master the technique by tomorrow. Perhaps Miss McCall has told you of the shooting contest? Oh, good. And of course I shall be happy to reimburse you for your trouble."

He waved that notion away.

"Time is, of course, of the essence. So if you are free, could we start immediately?"

His head seemed to be bobbing automatically.

"Excellent. Since I have, ah, left the impression with others that I am already a crack shot, I should like to be out of sight and earshot of the house. Do you ride, sir?"

The head was right on cue.

"Then let me suggest that we go change our clothing." She had found the club uniform excellent for fencing; he was still Harlequin. "Shall we meet at the stables in half an hour? I have a place in mind that should satisfy my requirements."

Less than an hour later they emerged on horseback from an area of woodland that cut off the view from Habersham Hall. She was wearing a dark gray habit, he, a brown riding jacket of indifferent cut, buckskins, boots, and the ever-present mask. Lady Lavinia led them through a grassy meadow before dismounting. "I think this is far enough away for the reports not to bother the horses," she remarked as she first watered her animal, then tethered it to a weeping willow that trailed its branches in the gurgling water. While her companion tended to his mount, she took an elegant leather case from her saddlebag and carried it back toward the wood. There she extracted a round paper target which she had placed on top of a handsome brace of dueling pistols. Worth joined her and stooped to examine the weapons. He reverently lifted one from its velvet bed to feel the perfect balance. "Ah," he breathed.

Lady Lavinia, holding a nail between her teeth, surveyed the wood, seeking the proper tree. She finally settled upon a large-trunked oak for the target. It was typical of her thoroughness that, rather than relying upon nature to provide the proper rock, she had brought along a hammer. She waved away Worth's move to do the nailing for her and accomplished the task with impressive efficiency.

Each took a pistol from the case, and Worth paced off the distance.

"I know nothing whatsoever about this." Her ladyship's voice was uncharacteristically humble. "We shall be expected to load our own weapons, I should think."

He nodded, then demonstrated the technique as she watched attentively. Her two friends would have recognized the fanatical gleam in her ladyship's black eyes. It alone in her studious demeanor betrayed her anticipation of a new and out-of-the-ordinary challenge.

The weapons loaded, Worth, with exaggerated motions that his pupil could easily imitate, lined up his shoulder with the target, slowly raised his pistol, took careful aim, and fired.

Lady Lavinia hurried to the target. "Bravo!" she called. "You have struck the center.

"Well, now, that seems simple enough," she said as she returned to take up her stance beside him. With calm deliberation she went through the preliminary procedure—then fired and missed the tree.

Worth's pantomimed critique was perfectly clear to his disgruntled pupil. She was closing her eyes and jerking her hand up as she fired.

The memory of the colonel's derisive remarks concerning females and firearms came back to haunt her. She gritted her teeth and stiffened her spine and tried again. This time she did hit the tree. Three feet above the target.

During the sword practice Worth had been impressed by Lady Lavinia's powers of concentration. But all that paled beside the focus she brought to this endeavor. A dozen more shots and she had hit her round piece of brown paper. Not near the center where her companion's shot held sway, but still upon the target.

"That will do. I think I have now mastered the technique well enough not to make a complete fool of myself."

In spite of a disguising mask, her companion had no difficulty conveying his astonishment.

"I know," she said ruefully as she took down the target. "I am unaccustomed to dealing in half measures. But in this particular instance I have no need to win. I am after another result entirely.

"Now then, Mr. Drury," she said after they were mounted, "I have taken up a great deal of your time. Are you sure that I cannot recompense you?"

He shook his head.

"Well, in that case, may I offer you a bit of advice?"

His eyes looked wary, but he slowly nodded.

"Tend to the roots of your hair, sir. They are beginning to be quite noticeable."

Chapter Twenty

PERSEY HAD NOT LEFT HER ROOM THAT MORNING. SHE saw no good reason to do so. The chambermaid had brought her tea and toast. Several books had been thoughtfully placed by her bed. She was deep into the pages of *Castle Rackrent* when a knock rattled her door.

"Come in."

Lord Worth did so and sent his mask sailing across the room. "One of these days," he observed matter-of-factly, "I am going to try to remove this blasted thing and discover it has grown to my face."

Her look was cold. "Is there any reason why you cannot remove it in your own bedchamber?"

He strolled over to stand beside her bed and stare down at her with folded arms. If he thought she looked particularly fetching with her nightcap framing her face and her dark hair fanned out against the pillow, his face was no more revealing than the mask. "Actually, I came to ask you a favor. But since you are still out of charity with me, perhaps another time would be better."

She closed her book and placed it on the candle stand. "That depends upon the favor."

"It's my hair. Lady Lavinia has just pointed out that the light roots are showing." He bent his head for her inspection.

She ruffled her fingers through the blackened locks, a bit longer, perhaps, than necessary for confirmation. "Grows fast, doesn't it" was all she could think of to say.

"Indeed." He smoothed it more or less in place. "I am a delight to my barber who, so I understand, owes his new carriage to my support."

She smiled, in spite of having determined not to. He grinned back his relief. "You'll do it, then?"

She was climbing out of bed, unconsciously revealing more of a bare limb than was quite decorous, a fact he did not fail to note. "I suppose I must if you are to continue your charade."

"Tell me," he said a few minutes later as he sat before the cheval glass, watching her dab black goo upon his head. "What do you think of Lady Lavinia?"

She paused to consider the question before attacking his roots once more. "I like her prodigiously. She has no pretense about her. Not like some I could mention," she added enigmatically. "Yet she is 'her ladyship' through and through. Also I would say she doesn't miss much."

"Don't I know." He squinted at his roots, which were now several shades darker than the rest of his hair. "I say. Won't that be as obvious as the other way?"

"It will be fine when it dries. Trust me."

"Haven't I always? But back to Lady Lavinia. I cannot understand what she is about. First she discovers that I can talk, then goes right on pretending that I'm a mute. Now she penetrates the rest of my disguise, yet I could swear that she has no intention of unmasking me. Either literally or figuratively. Am I a fool to think so?"

Persey locked eyes with his reflection. "Nooo," she said slowly. "I collect you are right. I can't say as to any other motives, but I do not believe she would jeopardize our production. For I am convinced that she is at least as committed as the colonel to its success."

"I see. And after that?"

She shrugged and restopped the bottle, then washed her blackened fingers in the basin. He ran a comb through his hair and winced at its discoloration. The streaked towels and inky water in the basin were equally distasteful. "I wonder what the servants have to say about all this," he mused aloud.

"Very little, I collect. They expect us to behave oddly. We're actors, after all."

"True." He stood up, slipped back into the coat he had removed for the treatment, then turned to face her. "Persey, we need to talk." His face was grave.

"Oh? And just what have we been doing, may I ask?"

"Seriously, I mean."

"And I thought keeping your identity secret *was* serious."

"Don't fence with me. I get enough of that with Lady Lavinia." They were standing close enough for him to reach out and touch her. He reluctantly rejected the idea. "There is something I must know. Do you love Piccolo?"

Whatever she had expected, it was not this. The surprise showed upon her face. "Do I love Piccolo?"

"That is what I asked."

She thought the question over seriously. "Why, yes. I had never thought about it in that particular way before, but, yes, I collect I must."

"Why *must*? That seems a strange way to put it. As though love were an obligation."

"Well, isn't it? No, I don't suppose you would know about that. In your station in life you've never had to face being out on the streets. Not knowing where the next meal is to come from."

"I'm beginning to face it," he said dryly.

"But you aren't a woman, are you? You cannot know by half."

"Granted."

"Piccolo has given me everything. My clothes, my food, my education. But most of all, he has given me a means of earning my living. So of course I am grateful. How could I not be?"

"I see."

"But it goes deeper than that. I am immensely proud to be associated with him as well. I doubt you have any real notion of his greatness."

"Why should you think that?" He was stung by the accusation. "I know something of his genius, believe me."

"Well, then you know more than most. For when outsiders—upper-class outsiders, at any rate—speak of the great ones of the theater, they are invariably thinking of the Kendalls and the Keans, their ilk. I am here to tell you that Piccolo has more talent in his little finger than any of your classical actors. Or all of them together, come to that."

"Down, girl." He held out a restraining hand. "I

said you did not have to convince me. I believe I have the picture."

"No, I don't think you do have," she replied thoughtfully. "For till you made me face it, I don't think I have had it either. I have never stopped to consider my own feelings for Piccolo, you see. And I do not think now that my high regard—my *love*, if you will—for him has a great deal to do with the obvious things I have just mentioned. I think it has more to do with the way he has cared. He has looked after me, you see—has put my interests above his own—has made me value myself because he values me. Oh, I am making a real hash of this. My regard for Piccolo is not something I can explain."

"On the contrary." He walked over to retrieve the mask from the bed and clap it upon his face. "I think you have explained it very well indeed."

He strode quickly from the room, closing the door firmly behind him.

Persey stared at the solid oak for several seconds, at a loss to understand why he appeared to have flown up into the boughs. Surely he could not be jealous of Piccolo. For if anyone had cause to be grateful to the comic, it was he. What other theater manager would have hired a green'un with a bogus set of acting credentials? Yes, his prickly mood was past all understanding. But, then, when had she understood anything about his lordship-cum-Drury-cum-Harlequin?

It was certainly impossible to reconcile the man she knew with the wellborn knave who had shot an acquaintance in the back. She thrust that problem once more into the recesses of her mind, where it had been lying dormant, to be dealt with at a more favorable time. But the problem that took its place was even more difficult to deal with: her feelings for the "wellborn knave."

For Persey now faced the fact that she was in love with him. If *love* was the proper term for the misery that engulfed her. It most definitely was not what she had been led to expect. Whatever happened to walking on air, dancing in moonlight? If this, indeed, was love, she, Persephone McCall, would gladly trade it for a good case of the grippe.

And what about him? she thought resentfully. How could he kiss her with all that passion and still pine after his gorgeous upper-class sapskull? But then a lowering thought strode in from the wings and took center stage in the theater of her mind. He had never actually kissed *her. Harlequin* had kissed *Columbine.*

"Oh, the devil with him anyhow," she muttered, turning away from the door to shrug out of her night things and don a walking dress. Introspection had never been her forte. Activity was her cup of tea. And it was time for the shooting contest to take place.

Chapter
Twenty-one

PERSEY WAS HURRYING ALONG THE PATH THAT SKIRTED the lake, when a voice behind her called, "Miss McCall! Do wait, please."

"Botheration," she muttered, recognizing the ladylike tones of the last person in the world with whom she wished to be. But by the time she turned to face Miss Hartland, who was hurrying toward her down the slope from the gazebo, Persey had rearranged her features into a pleasant smile. This was no small feat, for she had just concluded that Miss Hartland's blue silk dress and matching bonnet (French, she'd bet a monkey) made her own white muslin and chip straw look dowdy. "Are you going to watch the shooting contest?" she asked politely when the other joined her.

"Yes, I collect I might as well. Everyone else seems to be doing so." Miss Hartland's tone was peevish. When she had chosen the time for an as-

151

signation with Harlequin, she had not known where the contest would take place or that every resident of the Hall would be passing close by the gazebo as if the lake path were the king's highway. He, though, had obviously concluded that a meeting would be too risky, for she had seen him strolling along the path some distance behind Lord Newbright, his sister, and her friends, and followed at half the lake's length by the colonel and Mr. Warren. She had applauded the presence of mind that kept the actor from even glancing in the direction of the gazebo.

"I take it you do not care for guns, Miss Hartland?" Persey had fully noted her companion's tone of voice.

"I loathe the sound of gunfire." The beauty wrinkled her nose as they walked along. "But since gentlemen like to exhibit their skills . . ." She left the rest of the thought unuttered, too obvious for a waste of breath.

"Not just gentlemen," Persey reminded her. "This is really a battle of the sexes, remember? It was all Lady Lavinia's idea. She wishes to prove that men are not the superior beings they take themselves to be."

"But that is absurd."

"Is it? You surely do not consider males our superiors in all things?"

"Why, certainly. It is nature's law." The lovely eyes widened as she gazed at her companion. "And what woman would wish it otherwise?"

"Lady Lavinia, for one." Persey had bitten off a sharper retort. She redirected her attention to the group gathered around a tree, where a gardener was nailing up a target amid some discussion of the proper height. Trying to debate Miss Hartland would be fruitless at any time, she concluded, now least of all.

Some sixth sense caused her to glance to the left and spy Lord Worth some distance removed from the target. He watched his pupil with interest as Lady Lavinia insisted that the circle be lowered by one half inch. He was wearing the gray cutaway coat, trousers, and top hat he had traveled in. But now in contrast with his jet black hair and mask, the tall gray beaver looked several shades lighter than it had during the journey. Worth seemed to feel Persey's eyes upon him and glanced her way but quickly averted his gaze when he saw her companion.

Persey followed Miss Hartland to join the other two ladies who were seated upon the slope of a grassy knoll. After an exchange of greetings, Miss Hartland spread a handkerchief on the ground and sank down beside them.

"Shouldn't we move closer?" Persey asked.

"We thought it prudent to be well out of Lavinia's range," Jane replied.

"Oh, but that sounds disloyal."

"Not disloyal, *experienced*."

Addie was gazing farther up the knoll at "Mr. Drury." "Oh, Miss McCall," she said, "wouldn't your husband care to join us?"

"Your husband?" Miss Hartland's eyes widened. "Why, I had no idea that you were married, Miss McCall." She turned to follow Addie's gaze and her expression changed to horror. "You cannot mean— surely not!"

"Did you not know that Miss McCall and Mr. Drury are actually man and wife?" Addie's face reflected all the pleasure that knowledgeable people feel at others' ignorance. "She prefers to go by her original stage name. But if you don't mind my saying so, my dear"—she turned to Persey—"I think that is a mistake. I, personally, think that the Columbine-Harlequin romance takes on a whole new dimension when one knows it is not just play-acting."

It would have taken a Solomon to decide which of the young ladies looked more uncomfortable. Bright spots of embarrassment burned in Persey's cheeks while Miss Hartland looked pale and stricken. But Adelaide, having little in common with Solomon, did not notice. She started to rise. "Why don't I invite the poor young man to join us?"

"Oh, I am sure he would rather not," Persey said hastily, holding out a restraining hand. "Nothing personal, of course. But since his accident he is rather shy."

"So understandable," Addie murmured as sentimental tears moistened her eyes. "Still, I collect he might benefit from more society. But you know best, m'dear."

Her hopes rose as "Mr. Drury" chose that very moment to move to a new position that afforded a better view. To the observers he appeared unaware of the four ladies. But he still managed to keep his distance from them.

"Well, Lady Lavinia, shall we begin?" Colonel Hartland sounded a bit testy. "Are you quite satisfied now with the position of the target and our distance from it? We have changed both four times."

"Oh, yes, quite, thank you."

"Well then, you may lead off. Ladies first, you know."

"A cork-brained custom in most cases and one

154

that certainly has no application here. But since someone has to begin, I shall do so."

She stepped up to the mark, raised her pistol to shoulder height, and, with narrowed eyes, sighted, then pulled the trigger. The bark flew. Just above the target.

"Oh, my God!" Her brother breathed his disgust.

"You are aiming high, your ladyship," the colonel observed, trying with little success to conceal his pleasure. "But your bullet is on the line with the center of the target. Next time, perhaps. Now you, Lord Newbright."

The men all displayed credible marksmanship, but Mr. Warren was the clean winner, nailing the exact center of the target.

"Well now, shall we have another go?" the colonel asked heartily after he had removed the target, matching names to bullet holes, and the gardener had placed a new one on the tree. "Three best of five rounds, I think we agreed."

This time Lady Lavinia hit the lower right-hand corner of the paper, causing the female gallery, Miss Hartland excepted, to clap enthusiastically.

Lord Newbright's bullet took the center. "Bravo!" Jane shouted involuntarily, then reddened. His lordship, on the other hand, seemed pleased by the accolade, then struggled not to appear disappointed when Mr. Warren's bullet pushed his farther into the trunk. "Well done, sir," he managed to say.

When at last the contest was completed and the smoke had cleared, Mr. Warren emerged as the winner. Lady Lavinia was an uncontested fourth.

"I do not like to rub salt in your wounds, your ladyship," the colonel smirked, "but I think we have literally shot down your premise. The gun is not the equalizer of the sexes as you have claimed."

"Nonsense." Lord Newbright spoke up gruffly, to his sister's astonishment. "Proved nothing. Vinny had never shot a pistol in her life before yesterday, whereas I've been shooting ever since I got out of leading strings. And I wager the same could be said of you two gentlemen. Very credible performance, m'dear."

"Why, thank you, George." Lady Lavinia, quite uncharacteristically, colored with pleasure. "But allow me to congratulate you, Mr. Warren. You are certainly a crack shot."

"Thank you, your ladyship. But if you will forgive my saying so, a piece of paper is no test of one's proficiency with firearms. For that, one requires a living target. Then it becomes a true test, combining marksmanship and nerve."

"Hmmm," Lady Lavinia mused. "I think you are right. The example that springs immediately to mind is William Tell, who was required to shoot an apple off the head of his beloved son. Of course he was using a bow and arrow. And he was trying *not* to kill a human being, a condition that would, I collect, put more pressure upon a marksman than wanton killing."

"I certainly was not thinking along those particular lines, but I do take your point. Being required to come within inches of a living target would test the nerve as much or more than being compelled to hit it. In either case, if the hand trembles ever so slightly, the result is failure. Shall I illustrate?"

He reloaded his pistol while Lady Lavinia and the other members of the party watched, puzzled as to his purpose.

Warren completed the operation and smiled. There was something a bit feral in the baring of his teeth, but his tone of voice was light.

"Alas, Lady Lavinia, I lack an apple. But Harlequin's top hat should make an adequate substitute. "Oh, I say, actor," he called. "I wouldn't move if I were you." He raised the pistol and leveled it at Lord Worth who, about twenty yards away, had been on the point of turning to go back to the house. He now looked from the barrel of the pistol into Clarence Warren's face. Not for a moment did he doubt that his cousin would pull the trigger.

His instinct was to rush the other, but Warren seemed to read his mind. The pistol cocked. "Freeze, actor. We are playing William Tell. I am William. You are the son, who in my opinion was the greater hero, for he was required to have total faith in his father's marksmanship. How about it, actor. Think you can play the part?"

"Now, see here," Lord Newbright barked. "We are not amused, sir. Lower your weapon."

"Don't play the fool, lad. This is in poor taste." The colonel glared. Lady Lavinia did not speak. She simply looked from marksman to target with a scientist's detachment.

"Do stop it, Clarence!" Miss Hartland shrieked.

That particular command had a totally opposite effect from the one intended. Mr. Warren fired.

The top hat was sent spiraling off Worth's head. The noninvolved, with one exception, were frozen with shock. As for the actor, the mask once more served its purpose. But his lips were seen to snarl as he walked deliberately toward the gentleman with the smoking gun. His eyes sparked, flintlike, through the openings.

Worth's deliberation cost him. For at the sound of the shot Persey had dashed off her mark like a champion sprinter. With a choked cry she rushed the unsuspecting Warren and with all the strength

157

of an accomplished stage acrobat hit him a bruising blow in the pit of the stomach.

"Oof!" Mr. Warren doubled over.

Lord Worth, with nothing left to accomplish, gave the marksman a contemptuous look as their eyes locked. He then turned on his heel and left the scene.

"It is all right, m'dear." Lady Lavinia patted the distraught actress's shoulder awkwardly. "There has been no real harm done."

They had been joined by the other three shaken ladies. Miss Hartland's face was shocked. Her voice trembled with disapproval. "How could you have done such a thing?"

"Are you talking to me or to him?" Persey snapped. She was still suffering from reaction to her terror.

"Why, you, of course. No lady would ever behave in such a hoydenish fashion."

"Whereas it is perfectly proper for a gentleman to fire a pistol point-blank at another human being?"

"At a *hat*, my dear." Though he remained bent over, Mr. Warren's breath was gradually coming back. "I always hit what I am aiming at. Miss Hartland is right. Your reaction was quite uncalled for."

"It was no such thing!" Addie's voice squeaked with indignation. "Any *lady*"—she glared at Miss Hartland whom she was finding a most unsatisfactory romantic figure—"would feel exactly the same if someone fired a pistol at her husband. Still," she added as an afterthought, robbing her words of some of their initial weight, "I am not certain that many would have had the, er, enterprise to do what Miss McCall just did."

"What did you say?" Mr. Warren, fully erect now,

had been staring at the actor's retreating back. He shifted his attention to Mrs. Oliver, who was rather flustered by her previous boldness. It had now deserted her entirely.

"Well," she stammered, "I did think it probable that a lady might *feel* the way that Miss McCall did, but I—"

"No, no, not that," he interrupted. "Did you not just use the term *husband*?"

"Why, yes. Even though she uses the name Miss McCall, Miss McCall is actually Mrs. Drury."

His chin dropped. "You are married to the mysterious masked mute? Oh, I say. That sounded flippant. It is just that I am taken completely by surprise. I do owe you an apology, Miss McCall." He turned the full force of his considerable charm her way. "I can now see that my William Tell performance was in the poorest possible taste. But let me assure you once more, your husband was never in the slightest danger."

I wonder, Lady Lavinia thought.

And she kept the words strictly to herself.

Chapter Twenty-two

EVERYONE'S ATTENTION WAS NOW FOCUSED ON THE UP-coming performance. As the deadline drew nearer, the preparations took on an almost manic quality. Even Lord Newbright lost his detachment and pitched in to paint butterflies on bits of outdoor scenery, copying his own specimens to give verisimilitude. The cook and her helpers were creating mountains of almond, pepper, nun's, queens, and drop cakes for the reception that would follow the entertainment. The servants were sprucing up the Hall for the arrival of guests, and in their spare moments helping with the production in any capacity from makeup (the ladies' maids) to scene shifting (the footmen). The invitations had gone out, including several extended by various members of the cast to recipients not on the official list.

The acts outside of the Harlequinade, Lady Lavinia's province, had lately exhibited an alarming tendency toward expansion. Whereas at first her ladyship had been forced to apply pressure upon those with even a tidbit of talent to share it (Addie, for instance, was threatened with having to make her own way back to London if she refused to play her flute), now suddenly performance fever had struck and every resident in the countryside and nearby village seemed to have some skill they were eager to display. She was up to her ears in Morris dancers and glee singers and was finally forced to turn away several disgruntled auditioners. (Addie now stubbornly refused to step aside and make room for a fire-eater with blistered lips.)

Even Mr. Warren was not immune to the epidemic. He had at first been rather cool toward the notion of disporting oneself upon the stage, but he suddenly changed his mind and asked to sing a duet with Miss Hartland. Since he proved to have a pleasant baritone voice, Lady Lavinia was happy to oblige him. Also, as she later remarked to Jane, two solos from Miss Hartland seemed the outside of enough. It was Addie who suggested that the attractive couple be costumed as Romeo and Juliet. Adding a lute player (the village apothecary) and a crescent moon (carved and painted a bright yellow by the second gardener) seemed only logical at that point.

The couple was practicing downstage center when, for the first time, Persey and Worth referred to the William Tell incident. They were in their Columbine and Harlequin costumes, waiting their own turn in the wings. "They certainly harmonize well," Persey whispered, perhaps maliciously.

"Oh, yes, they are the perfectly matched couple." He had learned the art of scarcely moving his lips when he spoke. In spite of this hindrance, his tone was dry.

"They seem even closer after the shooting contest."

"Yes." He grinned suddenly. "I am sure that her sympathetic reaction to your attack made him all the fonder."

"I wish you would not mention that incident. I am trying to forget it."

"Why? I was most impressed. I think I have said this before, but it still amazes me that whereas other females only slap, you are much more resourceful.

"And by the bye," he added awkwardly. "I have never thanked you for that."

"There is hardly a need to. As Miss Hartland so unnecessarily pointed out, it was not an action to be proud of."

"No? That is a moot point. But I am grateful, for it saved me from discovery. In another second I would have drawn his claret. And I'm sure if I had come that close, he would have recognized me. Indeed for a moment there I wondered if he had done so. Fortunately, he had not."

"For the life of me I cannot see why you care one way or another if those three know who you are. Frankly I would not give a fig for their opinion." She kept her eyes on the performing couple while she waited for him to say that he had more compelling reasons for hiding his identity than a sudden loss of fortune. But once again he failed to take an offered opportunity to confide in her. He merely shrugged. "Pride dies hard" was his terse comment.

The pantomime rehearsal went well. The stage transparencies were the colonel's pride and joy and the tricks of construction worked like charms.

162

There was only one disturbing incident. When Harlequin made his entrance via the tightrope, then dropped from it center stage, the trapdoor opened beneath him. And had it not been for a remarkable display of dexterity that enabled him to catch the stage boards as he fell through and hang on by his fingers, he would have been seriously injured, perhaps killed.

There was a lot of wrangling and recrimination about who could have been so careless as to leave the trap unsecured, but no one admitted to any fault. In the end, Lady Lavinia appointed a stable boy to sit below stage at all times and make certain that such a mishap did not recur.

The morning of the performance brought Bedlam to the Hall. Lord Newbright prudently decided to avoid all the hysteria. Equipped with a large straw hat and a net, he was emerging from the east wing, when he hesitated a moment and then turned back. After a search he located Jane in the library, writing letters. A look of disappointment clouded his face. "Oh. I see you are busy."

She looked up and a smile erased ten years from her total. "It is nothing that cannot be postponed as well as not. Is there something I can do for you?"

"Not so much *for* me as *with* me. Don't mind saying that all these nervous performers are getting on me own nerves. Thought I'd get away from the butterflies in their stomachs and go out after the real thing."

It was so out of character for Lord Newbright to make a joke that for an instant Jane looked astonished before she chuckled. "What a famous idea."

"Oh, do you think so? Well then"—he reddened a

bit—"I was wondering if you would care to come along. That is, if your letters can wait."

"The letters most certainly can wait." She returned the quill to its holder and stood up. "I should be delighted to go butterflying."

"Ahrumph," said Lord Newbright, looking pleased.

Lord Worth was suffering a severe case of those butterflies which Lord Newbright spoke of. He tried to find Persey to ask what a performer of her experience did to quell them—if indeed she had ever suffered from such a malady, for somehow stage fright and Miss McCall did not seem to go together. After he had struggled through an elaborate pantomime to convey his quest, he was informed by the servants-cum-stagehands that Miss McCall and Lady Lavinia had gone out for a stroll.

Well, perhaps that is the answer, he thought. A long, brisk walk should have a calming effect.

Worth had circumnavigated the lake and was wondering if the next stage of his self-prescribed remedy should be a nap, when he saw a carriage pull up before the Hall. He was about to alter his course and avoid an encounter, when a servant opened the carriage door and Piccolo stepped down. Worth gaped in astonishment and barely stopped himself from hailing his uncle. Instead, he sprinted toward the coach.

At the sound of running footsteps, the actor turned. "Ah, Drury, I collect?" He looked pointedly at the mask.

The servant had moved away. Worth stood with his back toward the Hall but even so endeavored to keep his lips from moving as he breathed, "I desperately need to talk to you."

"You desperately need to learn to talk. Are you not taking the Pantomime a bit too seriously? Isn't that mask uncomfortable to wear on a stroll? No need to work yourself into the Harlequin role this early." He pointedly pulled a watch from his pocket and consulted it. "It is six hours till performance time."

"I live in the damned thing." The stiffened lips did not interfere with the bitterness. "And what is more, I am mute. This place is crawling with my acquaintances. Now, could we go to the gazebo? Please."

"Why, certainly." Piccolo turned toward the footman and raised his voice. "I shall stretch my legs a bit. If you will see to my portmanteau. Come, Harlequin."

"Have you learned anything?" Worth asked eagerly as soon as they were hidden from view inside the cool gazebo.

"No. Nothing helpful. Except that Sir Dibdin is mending rapidly."

"Famous." The words were only partly sarcastic. "It is only my character that is gone. At any rate, I won't be hanged for murder. Only deported for the attempt, I expect."

"Now, now, my boy." Piccolo patted him awkwardly on the shoulder. "Mustn't give up hope. We know you didn't shoot the cove. Which means there is someone else going about his business who did."

"Yes, but who? Plenty of people would line up to plant Dibdin a facer. But I can't imagine anyone putting a bullet in his back."

"Aye, there's the rub. And I'm afraid that he doesn't waver in his identification. It seems you were wearing a most distinctive coat, cranberry with silver buttons. He said it had been much admired and talked of."

"Good God, there could be any number of cranberry coats."

"Yes, and a lot of men with white hair—by the bye, your dye job is most professional. Persey? I thought so. But the combination of coat and hair—well, he does not waver. Now tell me of the situation here."

Piccolo listened intently, then shook his head in sympathy. "Circumstances have certainly contrived against you. And to think I believed I was sending you out of harm's way. Well, I should be getting on to the house. My hostess will wonder what has become of me."

But when they emerged from the gazebo, his hostess was seen strolling toward them along the lake path accompanied by Persey. As she spied the comic, the actress gave a glad cry and broke into a run.

"Piccolo!" She hurled herself into his arms. "I had no idea you were coming."

"Dignity, little one, dignity." The actor smiled down at her fondly. "This is no way to conduct yourself at one of the great houses."

"Bother the great houses! I wish I could leave right now. You will take me back with you, won't you?"

Lord Worth did not wait to hear more, but turned and walked slowly back toward the Hall. His performance butterflies had completely vanished, replaced by a dull ache in the region of his heart that was harder to define.

Chapter
Twenty-three

HARLEQUIN AND COLUMBINE STOOD ONSTAGE, PEERing through the curtains as the auditorium filled up. In addition to the invited guests occupying the gilt chairs, the common folk of the area thronged the parameters, crowding all the standing room available. Unseen by the actors, faces were pressed against the windows, with ladders enabling a few enterprising folk to see through the top panes of glass.

"We may seat more at the Wells," Persey observed, "but we've never been more packed. Oh, look. Lord Newbright has arranged for Piccolo to sit next to him."

The pride in her voice seemed odd to Worth till he recalled the social gulf that lay between his lordship and the premier performer of the day. "Has he now." He tried to sound enthusiastic when in truth he was blue-deviled past all reason. He gazed, as directed, over her head. But he was more conscious of pressing against her in order to see than of his gathering audience. "Where are they? Oh, yes, I see now." His eyes rested upon Lord Newbright in the second row. Mrs. Abingdon was on his right; Piccolo occupied the aisle seat on his other side. "Well, Piccolo's tailor is better than his lordship's," he quipped as he assessed his uncle's black and white evening clothes. "That is one up for— Oh, dear God!" His eyes had wandered to the row behind, where two men were just taking their seats.

"What is it?"

There was no answer. Persey turned to stare up at him. Thanks to the mask, only the grim set of his mouth gave him away. "What is wrong?" she demanded, shaking his arm.

"Oh, nothing really. I just saw someone— unexpected."

"Who, for heaven's sake?"

"No one you would know."

"Don't go cryptic on me. I have to perform with you, remember? And I am not up to doing that while at the same time wondering what has put you in a taking. So"—through gritted teeth— "who—is—it?"

"Sir Dibdin Kirby."

Her eyes widened. "The man who was shot?"

"The same. And unless I much mistake the matter," he murmured, perhaps to himself, "that's a peeler with him."

"A law officer? Oh, dear heavens. You must get out of here."

"Must I?" They were both oblivious of the increased activity onstage as Lady Lavinia put her minions through a last-minute check. "And just why would you suggest a thing like that?" he asked softly while his narrowed eyes impaled her through the mask.

"This is no time for games, *Lord Worth*." She spat out his name like an epithet. "Just get out of here while there is still a chance."

"How long have you known?"

"Since we first got here and the others were talking— Oh, what difference does that make? You must get away. Now, go!"

"And you've believed all this time that I deliberately shot a man in the back?"

"*They* said you did. They said there was no doubt. If it is true, I collect you must have had your reasons—or the gun went off accidentally—or something. For it does not seem—in character," she finished lamely.

"Thank you for that, at least." The need to keep his voice down did not disguise its bitterness.

"But what I believe or do not believe has nothing to say in the matter. Go!" She gave him a push in the direction of the exit.

"Walk out on a performance? What do you take me for? That would be more dastardly than shooting a gentleman in the back."

"Just leave," she snarled. "You have to go outside anyway to make your entrance. No one will think it odd. Then just keep going."

"And disappoint all of these folk?" He gestured toward and through the curtain. "Tsk, tsk! Miss McCall. And you call yourself a player."

"Piccolo can take your place."

"Damned if I let that happen. He may be the star of Sadler's Wells, but at Habersham Hall *I* am Harlequin. I'll never have this opportunity again. I am not about to relinquish it."

Behind them Lady Lavinia clapped her hands briskly. "Places, everyone," she called.

The orchestra broke into a sprightly if slightly off-key overture. The curtain parted. As the Morris dancers pranced onto the stage in a flutter of ribbons and a jingle of bells, there were whistles and claps and stamps of appreciation from the standing audience, mostly relatives. At its conclusion, their performance was rewarded by thunderous applause.

After that rousing beginning, the acts that followed were received merely courteously, with the exception of the Romeo-Juliet duet. "Reason Kneels to Love" was sung so sweetly that it caused the lute player to falter in order to dab his eyes. Even Persey had to admit, though grudgingly, that their duet would have been no discredit to the professional stage. Miss Hartland's beauty alone would have carried the day, she thought sourly, as (with Lord Newbright in mind) the couple sang "The Boy and the Butterfly" for an encore.

But it was the Pantomime that everyone eagerly awaited. The rest was merely prelude. And when the local juggler at last left the stage, rounding up his dropped oranges with the sides of his feet and kicking them before him as he went, and the curtain closed once more for the stage to be transformed, an expectant hush fell upon the crowd.

The orchestra struck up a pastoral tune and the curtain parted to reveal a sylvan glade. The audience at first gasped with delight, then broke into wild applause. Lord Newbright nudged Jane and beamed with pride. His butterflies were indeed beautiful in the gaslight.

The spectators had been too involved with absorbing every detail of rainbow (Addie's idea), wood, meadow, and swarming butterflies to notice Harlequin's assent of the rope ladder at the back of the hall. Then someone oohed and all heads turned to discover him poised upon the tightrope.

Persey, as she peeped around the proscenium arch, wrestled with two conflicting emotions: despair and pride. Knowing that his capture was now inevitable, she still was thrilled by how brave he was and how magnificent he looked.

Piccolo had brought along a new costume, especially made to his nephew's measurements. The background was of body-tight white silk emblazoned with diamond-shaped patches of vibrant colors, each one a time-honored symbol. Red for temper; blue for love; yellow, jealousy; mauve, constancy. All of these were outlined in spangles that caught the lights and sparkled like tiny prisms.

The audience held its breath. Harlequin began his walk. The rope stretched high above the center aisle and the spectators along its route leaned as far away from it as they could, ostensibly for a better view but in reality to be in the clear if the masked meteor above their heads came tumbling down.

Harlequin defied the law of gravity. His soft slippers seemed to glide above the rope. He danced. He pranced. He arrived at the center of the hall, only to reverse himself and return to his starting post with lightning speed and begin his progress to the stage all over again.

This time when he arrived at the middle of the rope, one foot slipped. The audience gasped in horror. He stood for an eternity, balancing precariously upon the other foot, swaying from side to side, his arms outstretched and flapping like a swan's while the terrified onlookers froze. And then he fell—

amid a collective scream—and grabbed the rope and cartwheeled around it several times before gaining a foothold once again and grinning down impishly at the audience.

They laughed delightedly, knowing they'd been gulled. He then ran lightly down the remaining length of rope and dropped onto the stage amid thunderous applause.

"Bravo! Bravo!" Piccolo himself called out.

And when the burly man in the row just behind the star rose to his feet, the other members of the audience thought it was the beginning of a standing ovation and almost joined him. But before they could put this impulse into action, his authoritative voice rang out.

"Jonathan Roderick Claxton Forsythe, Lord Worth, I arrest you in the King's name for attempted murder!"

Chapter
Twenty-four

A T FIRST THE AUDIENCE THOUGHT IT WAS ALL A PART
of the Harlequinade. Especially when the
burly man vaulted upon the stage with remarkable
ease for one of his girth. But when Harlequin removed his mask with a gesture of resignation and
Columbine came running out from behind the gathered curtain to hurl herself at the arresting officer
and pummel him with her fists, they began to wonder and to question all their neighbors. The mut-
tering increased as Piccolo leaped from his seat to
rush onto the stage and peel Persephone off the
cursing policeman's back. The Wells' star was followed by a pale young man who leaned heavily
upon a silver-headed stick.

Lady Lavinia took instant charge. "Just one moment, please." She addressed the burly man who
now had Harlequin in a viselike grip, preparatory
to leading him away. As the officer reluctantly

obeyed, she strode to the footlights and held up a hand. "Ladies and gentlemen, I regret to say that the performance must be delayed. I crave your indulgence as we alter the sequence of our entertainment. If you will follow Lord Newbright to the great hall, you will find refreshments laid out for your enjoyment. After we have straightened out this contretemps, I assure you that the Pantomime will be performed as scheduled."

She shooed out the orchestra (*sans* Addie, who refused to budge) and the incidental performers, leaving only the members of the house party who were gazing at Lord Worth as they might have viewed Lazarus, risen from the grave. Piccolo had an arm around Persey's shoulder, whether for comfort or restraint only he knew.

Lady Lavinia then turned to the officer. "Release him before you destroy his circulation entirely. In the first place, he is not about to run, and, in the second, he is innocent of the crime you accuse him of."

The intimidated officer did slacken his grip but retained his authority enough to answer, "Oh, he's the one all right, ma'am. No mistake about it."

"That's right, your ladyship," Sir Dibdin chimed in sadly. "Don't blame you for not believing it. Wouldn't have myself if I hadn't seen him with me own eyes as I fell. Of course," he added reflectively, "wouldn't have expected to see him walking a rope in tights and spangles either. Just goes to show how you can think you know a cove and—"

"Oh, for God's sake, Dibdin," Worth interrupted, "I did not shoot you."

"You didn't?" Sir Dibdin looked astonished. "But I saw you."

"I don't know whom or what you saw, but it wasn't me."

"It wasn't? Well, that is a puzzler, then."

The officer turned to stare at the accuser. "Surely you ain't going to take his word for it."

"Certainly." The other looked haughtily down his nose. "If Worth says he didn't shoot me, then he didn't. Word of a gentleman, you know. Couldn't expect you to understand. The thing is, though," he mused, "can't imagine who else could have done it. May not be the most popular cove in town, but can't think of anyone who would actually want to put a period to me." Even the attempt to imagine it caused him to look slightly ill.

"That, of course, has been the problem." Lady Lavinia had remained silent long enough. She now resumed command. "Everyone has been looking at this business all wrong. You, Sir Dibdin, were not the intended victim."

"You mean I was shot by mistake?" He brightened.

"No, not at all. But there was no intent to kill you," she added hastily as his face fell. "By the bye, what time was the duel set for?"

"Five." He shuddered for the ungodliness of the hour.

"Six, actually," Worth corrected him.

"No, it wasn't. Ghastly hour. Couldn't be mistaken. That's why I told my second to go on back to bed. I'd meant to apologize, you see," he explained to Worth, "for accusing you of cheating. I ain't myself, you know, after drinking too much hell broth." The other nodded. "Didn't suppose you'd want to duel any more than I did."

"You were alone, then, when you were shot?" Lavinia inquired, and Dibdin nodded. "The perpetrator was fortunate in that case that you actually saw him. I am sure he depended upon your second to identify the gentleman with the familiar coat and distinctive hair as he ran away through the trees. But even in your agony you still managed to note those crucial details"—Sir Dibdin cast his eyes down modestly—"and Lord Worth became a hunted man."

"But I say, Worth"—Dibdin's brow furrowed—"if you weren't the guilty party, why did you run away? If you had simply come and said you didn't do the thing, I'd have believed it. As it was, made you look guilty as the very devil."

"That is a very good question." Worth looked at his cousin speculatively. Clarence Warren was standing a bit aloof from it all, his arms folded and a half-smile on his face. "As I recall, it had to do with a quick attack on the arresting officers and a shout to take to my heels."

"And so you became the real victim of the duel." Once more her ladyship grabbed the reins. "The one intended to be ruined by it all along. The reason for your despicable behavior was assumed to be cowardice. It was concluded that you were afraid to stand at twenty paces facing a pistol. And yet when Mr. Warren here did his William Tell enactment, you neither flinched nor ran. Hardly the behavior of a coward. This discovery, by the bye, was an unexpected result of my shooting experiment.

"My sole motive for arranging the contest, you see, had been to discover whether or not Mr. Warren was capable of merely wounding, not killing, Sir Dibdin from so great a distance. For I found it difficult to believe that he would actually murder in cold blood to gain his ends. And of course he proved to be a crack shot. I had not expected to prove as well that Lord Worth is not a craven, though I was personally convinced of it."

"Are you saying that Clarence there shot me?" Sir Dibdin's jaw dropped. He turned to stare at Mr. Warren. "For God's sake, why?"

"Don't pay any attention to her ladyship's ravings, Dibdin. It's all a hum. A Banbury tale concocted by an ape leader smitten by a handsome face."

"Oh, the why is very simple." Lavinia was unruffled by the insult. "He wanted to eliminate his rival for Miss Hartland's hand. And *fortune*, too, of course. Though to do him justice, I collect he does love the pretty nin—er, young lady. But most of all," she mused, "I collect his motivation came from jealousy. Mr. Warren bears a decided resemblance to Shakespeare's Iago, or I miss my guess."

"But the identification," the colonel sputtered. "Sir Dibdin here *saw* Worth."

"Sir Dibdin saw a white-haired man wearing the coat of the gentleman was who supposed to be in that place at that time. The identification was inevitable.

"What I am certain happened was that when Mr. Warren accompanied Lord Worth to his lodgings the night before, he helped himself to the cranberry coat when no one was looking. It would have been simple then to obtain a powdered wig—a footman's, perhaps, or possibly a family relic from a previous generation. There would have been no problem either in restyling the wig sufficiently to pass muster. Then, after arranging for Sir Dibdin to arrive early at the chosen spot, Mr. Warren lurked there, shot him, was identified, then hurried away to awaken Lord Worth. After first restoring his coat to the clothes press."

"Fustian."

Mr. Warren's half-smile never wavered, but everyone else was staring at him with growing suspicion.

"There is one thing to be said to Mr. Warren's credit," her ladyship continued. "He did make sure that Sir Dibdin was discovered immediately. A cat's meat man informed Mr. Piccolo's detective that some 'gentry mort' had told him that a man had just been shot in the park. He had then slipped the fellow a crown piece to go fetch the authorities."

"Well, that was something at least." Sir Dibdin glared at Mr. Warren. "A person could have bled to death, you know."

"You surely aren't going to take this old harridan seriously, Dibdin. She hasn't a shred of proof, you know."

"That is true. Oh, I expect the cat's meat man could put you on the scene, but even that might not be enough for a court of law. But that is not my concern. My sole objective is to clear Lord Worth of the calumny. You will drop the charges, will you not, Sir Dibdin?"

"Most assuredly. And what's more, I will see to it that Warren here is struck off at White's."

"Oh, yes. A splendid notion. A fate worse than death." If there was any sarcastic intent in Lady Lavinia's statement, it went unrecognized.

During her ladyship's exposition, the colonel's indignation had been slowly mounting. It now exploded. "And I shall see to it that you are sent to Coventry, sir. Of all the despicable—knavish—dastardly— You, sir, are no gentleman." He turned to Harlequin. "Can you ever find it in your heart to forgive us, Lord Worth?"

His daughter's eyes were glowing as she gazed at

the young man in the silk costume. "Oh, but I must have known the truth all along. I now realize that I felt it when you kissed me at the tryouts. That is why I was so drawn to poor, mute Harlequin."

"Frailty, thy name is woman," Mr. Warren observed aloud as for the first time his bravado slipped and his face paled.

But Miss Hartland did not hear him. She was hurrying across the boards to throw herself into Lord Worth's arms.

Persey did not wait to witness any more of the tender scene. Her face was as blank as Harlequin's mask when she wheeled and left the stage.

Chapter
Twenty-five

A WEEK HAD PASSED BEFORE PICCOLO CALLED AT HIS nephew's house in Hanover Square. The hour was not early, but he found a rather haggard-looking Worth still clad in his dressing gown, drinking hot scalding tea and toying with the food upon his plate.

Piccolo readily accepted the invitation to join him for breakfast. "I must say you look like the very devil," he observed as he helped himself to boiled eggs and ham. "Been shooting the cat, have you? Celebrating the return of your good name?"

"Not really."

"Sickening for something, then?" He expertly cracked his egg and removed the top section of shell. "I received your note thanking me for my bit of help. Handsomely expressed. But I felt the need to speak face-to-face. I hope it is not presumptuous of me to call?"

Lord Worth reddened. "Don't be an ass," he snapped. "You know that the estrangement was none of my doing. You are always welcome, sir."

"I see." The older man chewed thoughtfully, then broke into his famous grin. "It does appear that the actor side of your family tree has proven superior to the noble side. But enough of that. I've come to ask a favor."

"Anything within my power."

"Oh, it's well within your scope. I want you to play Harlequin. At the Wells."

Worth strangled on his tea. "Are you serious?" he asked when he'd recovered.

"Quite. I feel I owe Colonel Hartland a performance. Can't afford to offend a patron, you know. The poor man was crushed after Persey walked out on us at Habersham Hall and the Pantomime was canceled—I had to entertain the audience solo, as it turned out. And by the bye, I cannot think what got into the chit, walking out that way. Most unprofessional thing I can imagine. Made her forfeit a week's salary for it."

"You did what?" Worth was glaring. "How could you?"

"How could I not? It is the customary fine for missing a performance. I should have raised it, actually, under the circumstances. This was a command performance, so to speak."

"You have not the slightest appreciation of her worth, have you?" His lordship was white with rage.

"Of course I have." The other calmly buttered a light wig. "None better. I think she will become one of the theater's greats. Another Mrs. Siddons. But she must learn discipline."

"The devil with her talent. I am speaking of

Persey as a human being. You have no appreciation of *that*."

His uncle eyed him thoughtfully. "You are wrong, you know."

"Then why don't you marry her?"

It was Piccolo's turn to strangle. "Marry Persey?" he gasped when he'd partially recovered. "The idea's obscene."

"Whereas," the young man sneered, "it was not obscene to make her your mistress? You, sir, are despicable. You clearly owe her the protection of your name."

"My mistress? Is that what you have been thinking?" Piccolo's shoulders began to shake. What started as a chuckle grew rapidly into side-splitting guffaws complete with tears that coursed down the lines in his mobile face. He wiped them off as he struggled to recover. "You actually think that Persey is my mistress? Well, that certainly explains a lot. And you, sir, are a fool. A trait that did not come from my side of the family."

"You mean she isn't?" Lord Worth's belligerence was bowing itself offstage. "Then what, for God's sake, *is* your relationship?"

"Hmmm. That's rather a poser, you know." Piccolo scratched his head thoughtfully. "Father-daughter?" He wrinkled his nose in distaste. "No, that makes me feel like Methuselah. How about guardian-ward? Ah, that has a much better ring to it. Not that she is, in any legal sense. But it has amounted to the same thing. For we have been together since she was two and her mother and I had a, ah, liaison." The performer's voice grew gruff and his eyes misted. "Georgette died three years later. She was the love of my life. And of course Persey and I stayed together. Nothing else to be done. I sent her to school—trained her for the stage—loved her like a daughter, I collect."

Lord Worth beamed at his favorite relative. His eyes were shining. "Oh, I see," he said.

"Well, it is about time," his uncle answered dryly.

"Would you look at that."

Addie, in the middle, simultaneously nudged Lavinia and Jane. They had arrived early at Sadler's Wells and were watching the theater fill up. They occupied the very same box Lavinia had reserved for Addie's birthday. Now their eyes were again glued on the one opposite. "Miss Hartland and Sir Dibdin. Who would have thought it?"

"You are reading too much into the situation, Adelaide," Lady Lavinia chided. "Of course Miss Hartland would come to her father's performance. And since Sir Dibdin had intended to see the Pantomime at Habersham Hall and was doubtlessly disappointed when it was canceled, it is natural that he, too, would come."

"But they are *together*. And I doubt they even knew each other before all that other business."

"That still does not mean—"

"Oh, I think it probably does." Jane did not often contradict her friend. "After all, Miss Hartland has run out of swains. Mr. Warren, I understand, has left to tour the Continent. And, after her defection, Lord Worth appeared to wish nothing more to do with her."

"For which I could hardly blame him," Addie sniffed.

"Nor could I," Lavinia agreed, "though I doubt her defection had much to say in the matter."

They were interrupted by a thunder of applause as the curtain parted. Then a dissatisfied murmur went through the theater when the patrons realized that the lecherous old man in his trademark breeches was not the Pantaloon they had come to see. But they were tolerant and even greeted Colonel Hartland's rendition of the star's "Hot Codlins" with polite applause.

Then all was forgiven as Columbine skipped onstage. Her low-cut bodice was made of white satin and sprinkled with tiny glass "diamonds" that reflected the lights and sent sunbeams flashing all around her. Her short skirt flared out in bands of bright reds and blues and yellows and greens. The basket she carried was filled with artificial blossoms of the same vibrant colors.

"Oh, how lovely," Addie sighed in one stage box, while in its opposite Miss Hartland gave Sir Dibdin an uneasy look as he inched forward upon his chair.

Persey felt as much as saw the movement and looked up through lowered lashes to identify its source. There wasn't time to decide whether she was relieved or disappointed not to see Lord Worth. For this was not Piccolo with whom she shared the stage. Colonel Hartland would need her undivided attention and support if he was to make it through the evening.

Once more she was Columbine. As her hips swayed provocatively, she walked by the older man with exaggerated indifference. His popping eyes followed her and the audience began to titter. She reversed herself and passed him by again, now flirting outrageously. Pantaloon clutched his heart. One hand mimed its accelerated beating. On the third trip he managed to clutch her hand; he then went down on one knee to kiss it. As Columbine bent over to aid him in this pursuit, Harlequin entered the stage on exaggerated tiptoe. He was carrying his "magic" sword, constructed of two wooden planks, joined at the hilt.

The audience held its breath as he reacted to his flirtatious sweetheart's infidelity by drawing back the sword. Its flat side smacked on Columbine's extended derriere with a resounding crack that sent her sprawling to the accompaniment of laughter. She raised herself indignantly and her eyes grew wide. "You!" she exclaimed, unscripted, and the audience howled again.

Harlequin had quickly switched his attention to his rival and was now stalking him ferociously around the stage while Pantaloon ran and shivered and jumped and fell, always just out of sword's reach until finally he escaped down a stage trap in a cloud of smoke, and Harlequin turned his wrath once more upon the quaking Columbine.

The chase was frantic. The audience rooted for the lovely Columbine's escape until it became blatantly obvious (as when Harlequin stumbled over a fallen log and went sprawling and she waited, foot tapping, for him to rise) that the jade actually wanted to be caught. And when she was and the man in the mask pulled her roughly to him, cheers and whistles greeted the confrontation.

The kiss proved worth the wait. Both of Columbine's feet left the floor, to the audience's delight. Harlequin's hat flew off. Columbine's fingers tangled in his black-and-white hair. And when she at last came to her senses and tried to extricate herself, he would not release her but took a deep breath and kissed her once again while box, pit, and gallery whistled and cat-called their approval.

"I do not think he is acting, do you?" Addie inquired.

"Oh, no," Lady Lavinia replied. "He is good, but not that good."

The lovers left the stage to tumultuous applause, and the moment they were out of sight, Columbine whirled upon Harlequin. "Nobody told me you'd be here," she spat out.

"Probably thought you would walk out if you knew, as you did at Habersham Hall."

"Well, you are right as can be there. I am utterly sick of playing with amateurs. That kiss was all wrong, you clodpole. It should be four beats and over."

"Oh, really?" He cocked an eyebrow. "It felt right to me."

"That is because you view the part of Harlequin as a mere exercise in lechery. Every time you put on that mask, you treat it as a license to make love."

"Hmmm." He thought it over. "You may have a point." He slowly removed his mask. "Enough of this Harlequin-Columbine charade. It is high time that Lord Worth kissed Miss McCall."

He proceeded to do so and topped his stage performance by several notches. She emerged, gasping. Her open palm resounded on his cheek like a two-planked sword.

"Persey!" He gaped at her. "You slapped me!"

"Well, what did you expect?"

"A kick in the shins. A blow to the stomach. A knee to—well, never mind. I had my guard up against any unorthodox counteraction. But I did not expect anything so conventional. Is that a sign that you are actually mellowing toward me? You surely must suspect by now that I am in love with you."

Her jaw dropped. "You are?"

186

"Hopelessly. And you?"

In answer, she threw herself back into his arms.

This time the lengthy embrace was interrupted by a preemptive throat clearing. Piccolo's nephew opened his eyes to see the world's premier clown glaring daggers at him.

"Oh, it's all right, uncle," he grinned. "The Viscount Worths always marry actresses. It has become a tradition with us, you see."

The audience was becoming restless. "Piccolo! Piccolo!" they chanted, stamping their feet.

And then they broke into cheers as the clown himself somersaulted upon the stage. "Are we here again?" he called and the audience responded, "Piccolo! Piccolo! Piccolo!"

Addie looked perplexed. "But that's not all of the Harlequinade, is it? Shouldn't there be more?"

"Oh, I suspect that Columbine and Harlequin are about to be caught in parson's mousetrap and their minds are not upon the stage."

"Are you implying that Mr. Drury—Lord Worth, I mean to say—and Miss McCall will be getting married?" Addie's eyes glowed.

"Most assuredly."

"Then why did you not say so?" Jane looked disapproving. " 'Parson's mousetrap' indeed. It is not like you to use cant phrases, Lavinia. It demonstrates a deplorable lowering of your standards. I shall certainly make a note of that lapse into the vulgar tongue when I record our latest adventure in the Pickering Club minutes."